A. A. Bavar

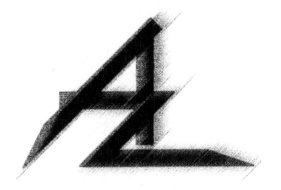

Az – Revenge of an Archangel

by A. A. Bavar

edited by Natalie Bavar

current cover illustration by Sarah Bavar

original cover art by Sarah Bavar

A. A. Bavar

SUMMARY

Can innocent love heal your heart even if you're the Angel of Death?

Azrail is an archangel, one of the original four. He's also the Angel of Death, the harvester of souls, the one who comes to your deathbed. But when a ruthless killer makes a deal with Lucifer and murders his goddaughter, the rules change and all hell breaks loose. Az seeks revenge and then narrates his story to the new face of death before succumbing to his fate.

Az is a fantasy novel that takes us through a journey of deception, rivalry, love, and self-discovery as narrated by the dark and edgy Angel of Death himself. It's a fast-paced, action packed story full of emotion, witty dialogue, and dark humor. Ultimately, Az is about an archangel who lost himself to humanity only to find himself again in his humanity.

For my lovely wife, Jennifer, my rock and beacon.

For my three wonderful children, Sarah, Natalie, and Navid, with love and admiration. If you ever need anything...

For my mother who is the epitome of fortitude and love.

For my father who just keeps on going and enjoys all that life has to offer.

A. A. Bavar

PROLOGUE

"The root of all evil is greed, and Man is defined by his roots."

Lucifer

A. A. Bavar

ONE

I am thousands of years old and have won many battles, but tonight I lost the war.

There was no defining sound of footsteps or rustling of feet, but I knew she was coming. She? Yes, I could tell by the subtle, delicate brushing of her bare feet on the cold, stone floor. "You're here sooner than I expected." I paused and allowed my voice to echo in the hollow darkness of the room, staring through the inky blackness at the even darker outline of the approaching hooded figure. She moved with eerie silence and was soon standing behind the oak table in front of me. "Are you committed enough to do this?" I asked in masked anger, even though I knew there was no answer to that question. It was not her decision to make. She had no choice.

The hooded figure did not move or make the slightest sound as she stood there in dead silence like a statue. How irritating. What the hell was she waiting for, a formal invitation? I angrily rapped my fingers on the table. "You want to take me now? Then do it! But don't think that I will be asking for repentance from you or anyone else; *ever*." Her job description, as far as I knew – and believe me, I did – didn't ask for much, just the willingness to be in the right place at the right time and offer salvation –

when she felt like it. If she was to be my successor, the new face of death, then she had better learn to be more objective, but she just stood there. Her tall, slender figure loomed in front of me, almost as if it were floating, and I wondered what she looked like. Was she young, serene and unblemished? I chuckled softly. Man would take care of that in no time.

I looked up at her impassive posture and suddenly burst out laughing. If I had lost my sense of compassion and empathy for Man at some point in the past few thousand years, I still had my sense of humor, and although dark and not entertaining to the dying, it was humor nonetheless. "Well, clearly you're socially handicapped, or just dumbstruck to see me. But lucky for you, your clients do most of the talking, weeping, and begging anyway." I stopped and scratched my nose. Nothing. "You're not a mute, are you?" Still nothing. "Okay, Missy. You want to start your job the hard way, be my guest. Want to be my confidant? Listen to my sad story? Fine, I'll take you up on that offer, but don't imagine for a second that you won't be my executioner." I stopped and squinted, fixing my eyes on where I thought hers would be. "Because you will *never* be my savior. Now, *sit!*"

I heard a soft crackling noise and glanced down, and although I couldn't see her hands, I knew exactly what she was holding. I would recognize that sound anywhere. "I *said*, sit." The robed figure gently pulled the chair back without making a sound and slipped into the seat. I smiled.

She had that part down pat. No dead man walking would ever hear her come.

"How does it feel to hold a dying soul in your hands for the very first time? Can you feel its history? The velvety veins where life used to flow strongly and freely; now brittle and coarse with nothing more to give? Can you feel *me* there in your hands?" My voice was low, barely audible. "It's ironic how the hunter ultimately always becomes the hunted. The thrill of pursuit turning into the despair of flight. The only difference here is that I chose to become the hunted and I have no fear."

Suddenly, a breeze swept the room and a faint shaft of light fell on the table across from us. The delicate fingers opened as the current snatched what was a withered leaf, and it slowly drifted down, landing softly on the dark, wood surface. I held my breath and closed my eyes. Some part of me did not want to see what I knew was inscribed on that leaf. In a blur, I saw the name of every soul that I had ever retrieved since the beginning of creation flash before me, and the finality of the moment – the result of my decision and actions that day, finally sank in. With a deep breath, I opened my eyes and looked down. To my surprise, the leaf was blank, the space usually inscribed with a name still empty. Then, before I could take a breath of relief, the defining gold letters slowly started to appear in script.

"Stop!"

The figure did not move, but the writing came to an abrupt halt right after the tail of the first letter; the letter *M*. I stared for a moment. *M* for Malak al-Maut, the Angel of Death; *me*! What the hell? Was I really ready for this? To give myself to Lucifer without even a final fight? Vanish from existence without anyone knowing why I did what I did? No, the robed figure had to know. She had to hear from me that my fall was not due to weakness. That it was exactly the opposite, a show of ultimate defiance and maybe, just maybe, that knowledge would save her. "This is going to take a while, so get nice and cozy."

TWO

I inhaled, the flow of air into my lungs deliberate, almost calculated, and let my chest expand to its maximum capacity as I pondered where to start. Then, as the pressure increased and I was forced to obey life yet again, I began.

"Sometimes, we stumble over the truth but still choose to ignore it because it's the easy way out; the weak way out. But how long do you really think you can fool yourself before someone comes along and smacks reality in your face?" I slowly slid my hand across the table and touched the edge of the leaf. I'm not sure what I expected, maybe visions of my past or feelings of remorse, but for there to be nothing was surprising. I pulled my hand back and continued, "And even if that doesn't happen, your memories will always be there to remind you, hound you as you try to make peace with yourself. Yes, it's true that time can take off the edge, make the bitterness of life less acute, but can it really heal you? No! At most, it can stone-wash the images that hide in the crevices of your mind and numb the feelings of pain and sorrow that are stashed away in your heart. But that's not enough, because there are moments that mark you, scar you, and are always present no matter how long you wait or how hard you try to forget." I sat up and leaned forward with my arms resting on the table crossed in front of me. I felt like a judge scrutinizing an already convicted defendant.

The hooded figure was rigid as a board, her back straight with her head erect and staring in my direction. I cocked my head, trying to see her eyes, but they were hidden under the brim of her hood. "It's these memories that fester and boil inside you until they get amplified to the point where they consume you; destroy you." Suddenly, I felt tired.

I shrugged and leaned back. What did it matter anyway? She was so young. What could she know about life and existence? She was Man turned angel; and I?

"When I think of it, even I can't say that I understand existence, but I do know a thing or two about life and death. I wasn't born from a womb – thank Father for that, but at some point I was simply there, and it was long before the creation of Man. However, it wasn't life as *you* experienced it. It was more like an ever present fog that washed over nothing and everything without a real reason. After all, what purpose could there be for me when there was nothing to be purposeful about? But Father changed that and gave me a physical body where I could move and interact, and I immediately became aware that I wasn't alone. I was finally *born* to my brothers and the world."

I brushed my hand over the surface of the table and revealed the cover of a book that wasn't there just moments before, *The Three Musketeers*. Interesting, I still had my powers.

"My favorite book, and definitely more enjoyable than the Bible."
I passed my index finger over the embossed letters of the cover, stopping
at the author's name. "Alexander Dumas! Ooh, I liked him. He gave us –
the four archangels – a lot more life and glory than we deserved, and I
enjoyed that. But the way he made us live for life and love was a fallacy." I
recalled something I once told Dumas in a conversation, and said in a
grave voice, "*It's necessary to wish for death, and see me come, to know how
good it was to live,*" and paused. As I looked at the dark form before me, I
wondered what kind of life she had and how old she was when I took her
soul. Would I even remember her? Did she ask for forgiveness? Man feared
me for good reason. For a person waiting for me, death is terrifying, never
funny, seldom enlightening, but always revealing.

"Dumas and I argued, but he still changed the saying and made it
eternal in his own way, and got it wrong as Man usually does. Life, with its
miseries and losses, is never good. Death, on the other hand, can bring you
peace." I paused. Nothing, no reaction. "Oh, so you want to know about
The Three Musketeers? Well, let me tell you. *I* wanted to call it *The Two
Musketeers of Heaven, the Newcomer, and the One Who Mucked it All Up*,
but I saw how that would make heads roll – Dumas's to be more precise,
so I let him keep his boring title as long as he got the story somewhat right."

I thought of us – the archangels, as we were in the beginning,
before Man, and my stomach muscles tightened. We were so different.
"For two of us, life would revolve around death; for the other two, it would

be more about service. Yes, the *three* in the title is somewhat misleading."
I reached down and in the dark felt the hole in the underside of the table
where a knot used be, and then slid my fingers diagonally to the left and
found the beginning of a deep gouge that ran towards the center of the
table. It was old, almost as old as Michael who had put it there, and I would
start with him.

"Michael was quiet and reserved, but with an intense energy and
when he talked, you listened. He was always ready to fight for justice and
defend Man and never blinked in the face of danger. And why would he?"
I stopped and chuckled. She would probably fall in love with him as
women do with hunky meat-bricks, or find him terribly demanding,
insensitive and unapproachable. "He was huge and way, way too big for
anything to scare him, and he designed and perfected every detail of his
armor himself. So, it was natural for Man to see him as a God, call to him
as the *Protector* and worship him like no one else."

"As for Gabriel, he would love you. You make the perfect audience
for his long-winded reasoning. I can't remember anyone, *ever*, not
conceding to him just to have him shut up." I looked to the side, almost
hoping to see Gabriel standing there. I loved him because he was the only
one who could calm me and make me see reason, *when* I allowed it. "You
know, that's not fair. He *was* infuriating with his constant calm and warm
demeanor. After all, Man misbehaves all the time and I wanted him to
react like I would – just *once*, and slap some sense into Man and make him

obey through sheer force and fear. But ultimately, his patience saved and guided Man more times than I can count." I grinned to myself and said, "The *Archangel of Truth and Judgment,* all he needed was his mouth and his comfy robe."

I was finally where I hated to be, and as before, my muscles tensed and I felt the adrenalin surge in my veins. I could see the reflection of my eyes on the shiny table surface, usually dark and deep, now glowing an electric blue. Even to me, after all these centuries, that was still cool and I surreptitiously looked at my devoted admirer hoping for a reaction; awe would be nice. Nothing. I guess I was too intense, probably even frightening with my disheveled and bruised look. I brushed the damp hair from my eyes and nodded to myself.

"Well, the boring part is over, 'cause now we're going to talk about," I paused pointedly as I stretched out the *ci* in my remaining brother's name, and hissed, "Lucifer." The thought of our explosive encounters brought a cynical smile to my face. "What can I say that the world doesn't already know? He was intelligent, handsome and, even then, the soft-spoken and politically driven one. In today's world, he would be voted *the one most likely to succeed.*" I smirked. "That should tell you something about Man and his tendencies. *Most likely to succeed* because you are the best in your class at being elusive, conniving and deceitful. And guess what, Father even named him the Day Star, or Day Spring of a new era; the promise of the future of humanity!"

I stopped and laughed softly at the irony of it. Still no reaction, not even a sigh or subtle shake of the head from the statue sitting in front of me. "Don't you see the irony of what is Lucifer? He is darkness, the destroyer of hope and yet his name literally means *bringer of light.* Damn, are you even listening?" As always, the thought of Lucifer unsettled me and engaged my anger. I abruptly stood up and in my frustration knocked over my chair. It was big and heavy, made of solid wood, and the crash was loud enough to make anyone jump; anyone except my new companion. Maybe she really was deaf. "He had no moral compass, and was a goddamn selfish, power-thirsty tyrant."

I remained standing for a moment, embarrassed at my outburst. Then, I picked up the chair in frustration and sat down again, never taking my eyes off of her.

"Well, we all know what happened to him. He defied Father and finally succeeded in having his own throne by getting his ass kicked out of heaven. And by the way, contrary to popular belief, it was actually Michael who confronted him and expelled him." I leaned back in my chair and put my feet up on the corner of the table. I wanted to look casual and unconcerned. Why did I even care what she thought of me? "That was a gruesome battle and I remember thinking – quite selfishly, thank God Michael's the protector and not me. Well, little did I know that from that moment on, I would be the one doing all the fighting where Lucifer was concerned. He was the Lord of the underworld, and with no souls to rein he was thirsty to get his claws into Man. And I, quite naively, helped him with that."

I put my feet back on the ground and we both sat there silently in the darkness. This was the last time I would be in my room, my sanctuary, and I wondered what changes she would make. I looked around, and even through that darkness, my eyes found every marker, scratch and scuff mark that defined my existence. I groaned in dismay. She was going to change it all and I knew exactly what she would do. She was going to make it cozy, warm and inviting until her soul told her differently and light and warmth became intolerable. Without warning, anger, rage, deception – I don't even know what to call it, would replace hope and she would hide in the cloak of darkness wishing she had never been born.

Strangely, I felt a pang of concern for her. "Are you aware of what you've done?" I can still remember how through the ages darkness slowly filled my senses and took over my soul, but no matter how I tried, I had no choice and unlike Man, had to obey. "You were unconquered, *invictus!* Why would you give that up? And for what? Don't you see the privilege that was reserved for you alone? To be the master of your fate and the captain of your own soul!" I hated that quote because it was a provocation, a jab at me. As I coached and mentored Dumas, so did Lucifer – for a brilliant instant, inspire William Henley. With a triumphant grin, I grabbed a strand of my wet hair and with a flick of my hand pulled it out.

It hurt, the pain shooting through my skull, but the control made me smile. "Today, *I* was finally the captain of my soul and the master of my fate."

My words were pointless. What was done was done and it didn't look like she cared anyway; but she would. Just like me, a long, long time ago, she was the newcomer and the path was already defined for her. I remembered my first mission as an archangel, the creation of *Adam* – the one who came from earth; Man created in Father's image, and sighed with lamentation. If only we could be born already wise to the world. Suddenly, my mind was on fire and images of that fateful day filled the darkness of the room.

THREE

Swords cut through the dim light, the red glow of the candlelight reflecting off the edge of their blades, the sound of clashing steel bouncing off the stone walls. It was a masterful show of strength versus agility as Michael and Lucifer tirelessly and with great abandon lunged and parried, doing justice to the future tale of the musketeers. And although the fight was not real, it was as intense and physically demanding as any battle that I would come to face against Lucifer in the future, with the exception that they were not in it to maim each other. I stood watching, observing Michael – the brute force of nature, attack the more polished and controlled Lucifer. I was in the corner of the room that would, unbeknownst to me, become the only place where I could seek a moment's respite from my obligations; the *somber room*, as Gabriel would come to call it. But it wasn't dark and dismal yet, and we were still brothers and united at heart. In an instant, however, that all changed.

Gabriel walked in as the two of them battled across the floor, blades slicing and swishing through the air. He looked calm as usual, but I could feel a sense of urgency in his demeanor. I motioned and he cautiously made his way to the corner where I was standing. He smiled.

"Azrail, Father has made up his mind. Today, we seek the dirt to create Adam!"

I looked at him bewildered. It was frustrating to be the newcomer, and Gabriel almost always forgot that I hadn't been with them as long and so didn't know much of what was going on. But I couldn't blame him. I quickly learned that in order to think, I had to tune him out because he was always talking, mediating or rambling on about something. So, it was quite possible that I had let this tidbit of information slip through the cracks. Thankfully, I'm pretty sure that he doesn't remember all that he's talked about in the past either; although it's pretty much *everything*. "Adam?"

"Yes! The creation of Man in Father's image," Gabriel said excitedly. "Our children to serve on the earth below."

Lucifer, as he dodged a mighty swing aimed at his head, chimed in, "Serve or bore to death with long-winded, philosophical monologues?" And then added in a more challenging and condescending tone, "A creation likening Father but with a will of its own that will be governed by *dam* – the blood that is common to every animal."

I knew that Lucifer was discontented about something, but this was the first time that he openly showed rancor and dissension toward Father. It was shocking, and I was confused but also angered by his lack of respect. Before I could object, however, Michael warned, "Brother, be careful with your tone. It is not worthy of you or us."

Lucifer deftly jumped on top of the large, oak table in the center of the room that I had made the day before. I cringed, hoping he wouldn't scratch the surface. "Why? Father made up his mind and we're supposed to serve this creature. Nothing I say will change that, but I don't have to agree and I will *not* serve under it!"

"Luicfer! You will, as will the rest of us." Michael, overtaken by anger, thrust his sword up slightly more aggressively than usual. But Lucifer parried the blow with a small dagger which he had unobtrusively taken out with his left hand and grinned.

"Now, now, Michael. Let's not lose our temper again," he said, and jumped off the table backwards just as Michael's sword came down hard where he had been standing, its tip gouging the surface as it slashed across.

"Ah… my table," I moaned in dismay.

With the table momentarily separating the two, Gabriel rushed in and grabbed Michael by the arm. Michael looked sideways at him and his eyes betrayed his thoughts. I could almost hear his mental groan, and although we all knew we were in for a discourse, he respected Gabriel too much to utter a single word and lowered his sword. I, however, couldn't care less. I had to redo the surface of my table!

"Yes, you are right. Man will be governed by earthly blood and desire. *But,* Father in his wisdom also gave Man the means to control the desires that live in blood. He gave Man *alef,* the teachings that will guide Adam and make Man great." Gabriel looked at Lucifer and smiled warmly.

Apparently, Lucifer was not in a listening mood either, and Gabriel's explanation was not nearly convincing enough. He chuckled and said, "*Alef* over the *dam*. That's amusing." And then, he fixed his gaze one-by-one on each of us and said, "You have no idea. You close your eyes to what is in front of you even here, in this room, and spin fairy-tales about the nobleness of what will be Man. In that, you underestimate the power in blood, the essence that sustains life and defines survival. Man will always choose life over death; self over service; himself over his neighbor." He lifted his sword and pointed it at me. "He's worried about his table, and you," as he motioned at Michael, "only care about Father's praise and your dignity. Trust me, Man will be no different."

Lucifer's cynicism shocked me. "But we can teach Man! Guide Man!" I looked at Gabriel and he nodded in agreement, while Michael stood silently observing with his eyes, his rage barely contained. "It's Father's wish. You can't ignore it."

"Like I said, I will never bow before such toy creatures made of clay." Lucifer held his sword up like the horizon that was splitting between us, bowed his head and then stowed it. "You can go ahead and try, but in the end even Gabriel will find himself with a dry mouth and nothing to show for it."

It was a breaking moment, the three of us on one side of the table and Lucifer alone on the other. I wanted to say something that would calm Michael but not in a way that would condone Lucifer's position. "Come on, Lucifer, we're brothers. Let's do this, and then talk about it when we're more calm." And added in a meager attempt at humor, "I'll flip the tabletop, it's no big deal. We must stick together!"

"Must? That's an interesting choice of word." Lucifer pursed his lips, his eyes, lines of pure displeasure. "I think that we are at the crossroads of what is creation, and I will not be a part of it. It seems to me that the next time we meet I'll need my sword and it won't be for play." With that, he nonchalantly flicked his dagger at the table. It sank into the center of a knot resembling a bull's-eye with a resounding thud as he disappeared.

FOUR

The world below us was in creation. Earth, water and fire collided, tore at each other and exploded as the continents ripped and split apart. It was a vicious and unmerciful show of power, a reminder of what was in charge. Explosions sent melting volcanic matter into the air in every direction like red, smoldering spears as plumes of hot smoke rose around us. Mother Earth roared continuously through the chaos and destruction making talking an impossibility. The view over the intense physical assault, however, was breathtaking. I looked down and one thing was clear. Through destruction comes transformation and change; a change that I was not fully ready for.

Michael, Gabriel and I hovered at the peak of a newly formed mountain, its jagged edges razor sharp and steaming. None of this seemed to faze my brothers as they looked on unconcerned, ready for duty. But not me. Maybe they didn't take Lucifer's threat seriously, or took it as something that he said in the heat of the moment. But I didn't think so. Lucifer never said anything that he didn't mean, and he always followed through. And if I knew that, then Michael and Gabriel did, too. The turmoil below reflected my feelings. What was it that was tearing us apart? Was it us or Lucifer? Maybe he would reconsider.

"Hey, I said we're going in," shouted Michael, as he grabbed me forcefully by the arm. "Gabriel will get the clay and I'll go as protection. You stay here and keep watch."

I stared at Michael blankly for an instant. His voice sounded like a strange rumble and the words didn't make sense. But then it hit me and I felt a wave of resentment and anger. "Stay here and watch? Watch what?"

Michael moved closer and with his mouth practically in my ear, yelled, "I said *keep* watch! Not watch us. Gabriel talked to Father, so he should be the one to go in – and, he's the better negotiator."

With that, Michael tapped Gabriel on the shoulder and they dived toward the inferno below and were almost immediately swallowed by the smoke and ashes that filled the air. I knew what Michael wanted me to watch for; Lucifer. I guess he was just as concerned as me that he would try to stop us. Us? Not yet, not for me.

I twisted my head around in frustration and decided to move a bit higher, away from all the noise and heat. In my gut, I felt robbed of the chance to show my brothers and Father that I was ready.

"Not fun to be left out, is it?"

I heard Lucifer's silky voice without any trouble, and the manner in which his tone slithered through my mind sent a shiver down my spine. It was like it was in my head. I quickly spun around, but he wasn't there.

"Oh don't worry, *brother*, you won't be seeing me down there. I'm bored with all this and love my wings too much to subject myself to Mother Earth's nasty tantrum. You don't seem too happy yourself."

"What do you want, Lucifer?"

"*I* don't want anything. But you do."

Lucifer had an uncanny ability to read me, and it was unnerving. It was true that I wasn't happy and wanted my own space and the respect of my brothers, but I knew that would come in time. I would get my chance. What I didn't know, was that to spot a snake, you had to be a bit of a snake yourself. I tried to close my mind and push him out, but he was too strong.

"You're nothing but a shadow to Michael and a simple apprentice to Gabriel. Come join me and be your own Lord. There will be a big world for us to command!"

"What?" Lucifer's offer was an insult to me; a piercing betrayal. Why did he even consider that I would agree when this made it clear that the rift was with him, within himself? Did he really believe that I would desert Father and forsake my brothers for a title? If nothing else, I had integrity, and he would have to answer to Father for this. "Never!"

"Yes, I heard your whiny mental speech, but I'm not answering to anyone. Not anymore. Not ever."

Suddenly, the world underneath ruptured, opening a gorge filled with a glowing fiery mass. Michael and Gabriel shot out, expelled like insignificant little fireballs completely covered with soot. Worst yet, their wings were singed and black. I folded mine behind me and dived, sunlight reflecting off my bleach white feathers and gold trim. I was determined to succeed where they failed. Then, Lucifer would have to contend with me.

To my surprise, the opening started to shrink immediately, and I was too far to make it in time before it closed, but I wasn't giving up. Michael and Gabriel were right below me waving their arms frenetically, signaling me to go faster, as I spiraled down with maximum speed. I had never flown with so much intensity, but it still wasn't going to be enough. And then I got it, they weren't urging me on, they wanted me to stop! What, they thought I couldn't make it because they failed? I tucked my arms and wings beside me as tightly as possible and twisted my body into a corkscrew dive; it was all or nothing extreme diving. Everything became a blur as I shot down towards my target. The exhilaration made me forget about myself, and I thundered past my burnt brothers straight into the heart of the chaos. It was like hitting a stone wall. The explosions were bone crunching, and the intense heat burned my wings as I crashed through invisible shockwave after shockwave, but it didn't matter. Nothing mattered. My brothers hadn't made it past this point, but I would. I was going to succeed.

With a final push, I smashed through the molten crust, my muscles screaming in pain as my skeleton almost shattered from within. Fire and lava attacked me from every direction, burning and scorching my body as I thrust my right hand into the melting clay, but when I pulled my fist out it was empty. The skin on my hand and fingers was charred and blistered, but I tried again and again, and was denied every time. I looked down at my right hand and could see the white of bone and the horror of the abuse made me cry, the pain unbearable. "*Why? Why are you denying me?*" I switched hands and stubbornly tried once again without success. There was no way, I had to stop. I was burning alive and my wings were reduced to nothing but their skeletal frame. "*Mother, help me!*"

Suddenly, I felt an unusual cool and there was no more physical agony. I was floating in an ethereal state, and it reminded me of my existence before I was born into my body. It felt good to be disconnected from the material world, and if this was death, then I welcomed it. But I knew that it wasn't. I'm not sure why or how, but *she* had accepted me, and I had become part of something bigger. *Life* was not something to take for granted, and she had made that clear. But that wasn't all. She wanted something in return, a guarantee that her investment in Man was not in vain and that Man would remember and respect her. It required commitment – my commitment, and compromise from Man. I thought that I understood, and as the words left my mouth I reached down and grabbed a fistful of clay, "*... earth to earth, ashes to ashes, dust to dust ...*" It was a contract, forever binding, and a commitment to Man that would test and eventually destroy me.

FIVE

I thought that my return to health would take a long time, and was especially worried about my hand and wings. After all, I was never hurt before and this time managed to cause myself intense damage. The image of my hand and fingers, the skin reduced to charcoal and the sight of my bare bones was something that haunted me when I closed my eyes. To my surprise, however, my recovery was astonishingly quick. More impressive, yet was my transformation. I looked older, more mature and my new wings were jet black with a royal blue sheen and silver tips. Even my eyes now had a blue glow to them which reflected the intensity of my mood and made me look more unearthly. It all made me feel more distinguished, and although not what we consider a heavenly quality, my heart filled with pride, and for a fleeting moment I thought of myself as *The Angel of Life*. That's what I had become; I had found my place with my brothers. But almost immediately, my gut told me that I was wrong, and Father proved it.

I'm not sure what I expected to happen when Father finally called to me. A glowing orb of yellow light surrounding me and trumpets sounding as I drifted to heaven with my prize, who knows? I was young, proud and wanted a pat on the shoulder for a job well done. No thoughts of *service is what you do as an angel* even hinted to cross my mind. I wanted recognition from Father and the respect of my brothers. But what came next was shocking and a true lesson in humility. How ironic that I was right about my title, but mistaken about its context, for in reality, I had become the *Angel of Death*. That was my reward for accomplishing the one task that the other archangels had failed to do. Father gave me his most prized possession, the soul of Man to guard and care for. However, I didn't fully understand the significance of it or what that title really meant. But Lucifer did, and I soon felt its weight crash on my shoulders and almost break me on Mount Qasioun.

SIX

I was young and full of energy and felt more invincible than ever. After all, I triumphed where my brothers failed and it felt good; even if momentarily I chose to forget about Lucifer and our conversation. I remember strutting about with a stupid grin on my face, thinking how intimidating and cool it was to be the *Angel of Death*. But what did I know? What did any of us know about life and creation?

We were so naïve. That is, all of us except for Lucifer. Michael didn't say much, but I could tell that he was excited and anxious to serve and protect. As for Gabriel, he spent the days philosophizing about the wonderfulness of creation and spun visions – or should I say dreams, because although founded in truth, they were mere illusions – of a majestic, harmonious, and unified civilization that lived to serve and venerate Father. I shared that vision, Man created in the image of Father with holy attributes, and saw myself as the gatekeeper to his soul. But Lucifer had his own plans. His vision was quite the opposite and he didn't lose any time in putting it into action. Basically, we were gunning for the same trophy and he had the edge.

The Tree of Life, with the souls of the living as its leaves, was the central piece of that illusion. In my mind, it was full of enchantment and had a celestial aura that soothed any beholder while inspiring humbleness. That was because I had never seen death and, consequently, had never stopped to think about it; but in the back of my mind it would be noble and dignified. How wrong could I be?

Standing in Father's garden on that fateful day, I was overwhelmed and confused. My eyes were fixed on a brown and withered leaf that was on the ground under the Tree of Life. It was my first encounter with death, and it was way too soon; and as I would soon realize, way too wrong. I walked to the tree and slowly kneeled down. I could hear my heart pounding in my ears as a strange coldness took me over. What I would have given at that moment to rescind my position. Slowly, I picked up the leaf. As we made contact, there was a flash of golden light, and the name of the person whose soul I had to retrieve appeared on it. I felt sick to my stomach as my heart fluttered in my chest.

"How Father? How can this be?"

SEVEN

The Syrian sky was clear and magnificently blue, the sunlight warm and comfortable on my skin. It was my first time back on earth after that iconic day when I faced Mother Earth, and once again I was alone in my journey. It was a goddamned lonely job when it was time to do the dirty work. Not that I knew any of this then, but then age and wisdom can also be a curse. Time had no meaning or essence for me; it could be a day, a century or a thousand years and I wouldn't know it. Every image, every memory, was as fresh as the moment it happened and I had to deal with it no matter how I felt or what I thought. My feelings this time, however, were very different. Gone was the excitement of the challenge, the adventure, an opportunity for recognition, its place now filled with a mixture of fear and revolt. I didn't want to be there, and surely, didn't need to prove anything to anyone. But this was the job that I had anxiously signed on to do, and today was simply my first day at work.

The dirt path ahead of me, the only road to the village of Damascus, was a one way street to the beginning of a new destiny. I stood there and watched the beautiful blue sky – the golden ocean of chest-high wheat shoots, and the gentle breeze that caused them to sway in harmonious waves, with as much abandon as I could muster because this view would never be the same. I looked down at my silver tunic with its accented gold trim, my jewel studded leather belt and sandals, and my white and silver cape trimmed in black; and suddenly, I was furious. How could I look so clean, so alive and serene when death was laying around the corner? Didn't Father care? Didn't Mother care? Didn't life care? Could I be so callus and selfish to give up? No! If this was to be the suicide of life and nobility, then the wheat fields needed an eternal marker. With that, as if on cue, a murder of crows suddenly appeared and for an instant the day turned black. I focused on one and as it flew past saw the white pinpoint in its eye and for a fleeting moment, the whole sky was covered with white starry dots. I smiled and looked on as they flew overhead, following the path through the fields of wheat, painting an image that remained solely with me until Man did it justice; and he did. My decision was not in vain. I had to go on.

     I knew exactly where to find the body, but I wasn't ready to simply appear there and face the unknown. I wanted to think about it, plan the proper way to retrieve my first soul and fulfill my contract with Mother. There was no precedent, no one to learn from, so it was all on me. And the fact that I was about to start a tradition that would last as long as Man existed didn't make it any easier. All I knew was that it had to be noble and dignified. I decided to walk and let my mind process what I had to do. I imagined the body laying neatly on the ground, with a face that was peacefully serene as if in a deep sleep and waiting for me. I was so wrong.

Soon, I came to a narrow dirt trail that cut through the fields and headed west to the hills and Mount Qasioun beyond. I stopped and looked up at the mountain, it wouldn't be long now. Suddenly, a lonely crow hopped out from the field onto the road ahead of me, and for the second time that day I was staring into the tiniest light within darkness. It almost seemed like it wanted to guide me and started to hop along the path. I followed it and within a few steps – much sooner than I had anticipated – there it was, in an unceremonious display of barbaric violence, the most unimaginable and horrific scene. I gasped and stopped as my eyes fell onto a misshaped mass, and although I knew what it was, my mind refused to comprehend. A bloodied corpse, garmented only with a loin cloth, lay in a contorted heap on the path. It was the grown body of a young child who I had watched so often as he played in the fields and grew to be a righteous, young man. It was the body of Abel, son to Adam and Eve and brother to Cain.

I shut my eyes, but my mind was determined to keep the image of death alive and displayed it in minute detail on the black canvas of my mind. My head felt light, somewhat disconnected from the rest of my body, and my ears buzzed incessantly. I heard a repetitive rasping sound and in my detached state, it took my mind a while to realize that it was the sound of air entering and leaving my lungs as I breathed. Suddenly, my body was burning, and I was aware of every bead of sweat that was on my forehead. If I could think clearly enough to define it, I would call it an out of body experience; but maybe I really *was* floating. I grabbed my temple with both hands in an attempt to keep my head from swaying and slowly opened my eyes. Nothing had changed. The day was still bright with sunlight, and Abel was still dead. With great difficulty, I forced my trembling legs to take me to his mutilated corpse. As I stood there and looked down, my whole body started to quiver and then shake uncontrollably, and before I knew it my legs buckled and I fell, landing hard on my hands and knees. The earth, just inches from my fingers, was drenched in blood, and I could smell its metallic scent. I shifted my gaze from the bloody dirt to Abel, but what was I looking at? I had never seen death, let alone a gruesome execution like the one splayed before me. Abel's neck was cut all the way across, leaving his head almost completely severed from his body. My chest tightened to the point where I couldn't breathe and I thought that it was going to crush my insides and implode right before I threw up. My head spun as I retched again and again in between painful gasps for air, until finally, the world around me faded into a hypnagogic haze. My eyes went black and I heard the chilling, animalistic scream of a murderous beast. I thought I was also going to die when I realized that the screeching beast was me.

I don't know how long I lay there, but when I opened my eyes, Abel was staring at me. I felt a cold shiver and scrambled to my knees, and although I tried to look away I could not take my eyes off of Abel's. We stared at each other for a hauntingly long time, the magnetic attraction between life and death. I can see his eyes looking at me today as I saw them then, an expression of surprise, disbelief, even awe. I didn't know anything about death then, but it was clear to me that for Abel it had come unexpectedly and quickly. I reached over and with a tremulous hand closed them. His skin was cold.

"A terribly horrid scene to witness."

The voice came from behind me. It was an unexpected intrusion and the sound made me jump skyward with such intensity that my wings snapped open and immediately enveloped me like a shield. I turned and looked down, even though I knew who was standing below. I took a breath and landed with a thud in front of Lucifer. His appearance, as usual, was dazzling. His robe was covered with golden details and precious jewels, and he looked handsomely unperturbed and calm.

"What are you doing here? What do you want?" I said, my tone much harsher than I intended. But I was angry and embarrassed at my reaction, and he looked so unaffected and uncaring that I felt justified.

"I don't want anything, brother. Just thought I could help." Lucifer smiled in sympathy, but his eyes betrayed him. He was there to gloat. He had never accepted Man and every opportunity to prove his point was an opportunity that he couldn't let pass. If he only knew that these moments were not rare in the least, maybe he wouldn't be so keen to be there every time Man strayed. But – and I somehow always knew this – he had to be there because he was the reason for Man to stray.

"I don't understand what kind of animal could do this!" As the words left my mouth, I immediately regretted it. The statement was just an expression of my disbelief, but voicing it was a mistake. I had seen the cut and knew that it was not from a wild beast. The perpetrator was far more ruthless and insensitive than any animal; it was Man. But who? It didn't matter, because Lucifer would make sure that our encounter was anything but pleasant. With my compliments, he had the ammunition that he would use against me, to goad me. It's frustrating how I always did that, let my anger get the best of me where Lucifer was concerned.

"You're wrong. It was not an animal, brother, or at least not an animal in the traditional sense." Lucifer paused, and the grin that appeared on his face was of pure satisfaction. It was annoying, but worse yet, I saw how he savored the moment. "Look around, what do you see?" asked Lucifer, as he shifted his position and took a step closer to Abel's body, all the while keeping his eyes fixed on me.

I looked from side to side, my eyes sweeping the area, but all I saw was the vast expanse of wheat. With Lucifer, it was always a battle of wits, a test, a challenge to see who's better, stronger, superior. Why couldn't he tell me and get it over with? I hated playing games. It only served to get me angry and in this case, anxious. My jaw muscles were beginning to hurt, and if I gritted my teeth any harder they would shatter, but it was the only way to contain my frustration. I momentarily closed my eyes and took a deep breath, suppressing the urge to lash out. I would not let him manipulate me into losing my temper, and as I relaxed a bit, I noticed the crow standing just beyond Abel and a bit to the left. Was it trying to tell me something? I strained my eyes, but all I could see was wheat. I slowly turned and stared at Lucifer.

"I don't see anything. What am I looking for?" I said in a controlled, almost resigned voice. "If you know, why don't you just show me?" I was keeping my calm, but it was a facade, because I really wanted to jump and pound him to the ground. Thinking back, I'm sure he knew it, too.

"As you wish," he replied, "but I truly didn't want to be the one to do this." His silky voice could not mask the subtle condescension in his tone. He was enjoying every second of my discomfort. Without looking, he lifted his right arm and pointed. Then, suddenly, as we stood there staring at each other, a thunderous flash of red lightening exploded from his hand and flew through the air to where I had been staring moments before; the crow, now gone. The reflection of its blindingly reddish light off a metallic object was unmistakable.

I jumped back in surprise, my whole body a tangle of nerves. I glared at Lucifer, but there was nothing to say. I turned and walked to where the object was and picked it up. It was a scythe, its blade covered with blood. In all my existence, I had never experienced such overwhelming feelings of confusion, anger and helplessness.

"This cannot be!" I shouted in true disbelief. "This scythe belongs to Cain." I spoke the last phrase in a whisper, almost to myself. I had no doubt that Lucifer was somehow involved and my feelings of helplessness and confusion led to utter fury. I gripped the handle of the scythe in both hands with such force that my knuckles turned completely white and the wood started to creak under the pressure. There would be accountability; now! I turned to face Lucifer with such speed that the motion caused the scythe's blade to cut through the air with a loud and menacing *swoosh*.

Lucifer didn't seem a bit bothered or impressed by my outburst. Actually, it was my previous calm that was unnatural when he was involved. And although it had been an illusion, I had managed it for a short while. But now, we were home and in his territory. He gallantly stood there with his paternalistic wisdom and looked down at me. I stared back, the scythe held across my chest like a weapon, poised ready to strike. I wanted him to challenge me, engage me somehow, and maybe show remorse, anger, fear, anything at all! But his face was blank and unperturbed. He was a sadist and enjoying himself as usual.

"What have you done?" I shouted, "Tell me!" My grip tightened even more around the handle of the scythe, and the creaking stopped as my fingers dug into the wood and left their imprints.

Lucifer chuckled and said, "I didn't do anything," and tilting his head to the side while holding his hands up matter-of-factly, continued, "Cain was there, I was there, and Man showed his true nature. You shouldn't be surprised." I didn't know what to say, so I just stared at him and hated him for his cavalier attitude. What the hell – but that would come later. I believe that my look of disdain and contempt must have touched him – it would be the last time, but Lucifer surprisingly abandoned his arrogant attitude and, now I see too late, reached out to me. His tone was cool but sincere, "I just wanted you to see why this creature of clay is not worthy of our respect or loyalty. They have the one thing that we as angels do not, and they use it haphazardly and with disregard just because they can, without any thought to their so-called nobility."

But I wasn't listening. Not to Lucifer or even my own heart. The anger and disgust that I felt completely shrouded my judgement. I was caught up in the impossibility of Cain having done what he had done through his own volition. For me, free will did not exist, so for Man to use it in such an abhorrent and animalistic manner was incomprehensible. What I didn't know was that Man and his free will would continue to challenge me at every turn throughout history, and that would eventually extinguish my sense of compassion. So, as much as I hate to admit it, Lucifer was ultimately right about Cain that day. I, however, was blinded my naiveté and simply didn't know Man. What I said, and more importantly did next, sealed our fate and the last chance we had at reconciliation was lost forever. "So you admit that it was you who did this," I spat, "just as you did in the Garden with Eve! What trickery did you use this time to make Cain commit this heinous act? Explain yourself!" I was distraught and it felt good to unload. Lucifer had to be responsible. But, if there was the slightest possibility that Man alone was capable of perpetrating such a horrific act, then everything that I believed in would be a lie and Lucifer was the better of us. That, I could not accept.

Lucifer stepped back and took a deep breath. "Azrail, how can you be so blind? Listen to me. I did nothing but make Man become aware of his own desire and lust," said Lucifer, a thin gaunt smile forming on his lips. "Free will took care of the rest." I guess Lucifer just couldn't help it, he had to be himself. He knew how to push my buttons and couldn't resist. Either way, I wasn't listening and had enough. If there could be redemption for Cain, I would get it. I jumped the distance to Lucifer, bringing the scythe down in a lethal arc as I landed in front of him. Lucifer sprung back and lifted his hands in a gesture of peace, but it was too late. Blinding sparks flew from where the scythe's blade, covered with Abel's blood, cut deep into the flesh of Lucifer's forearm. Abel's blood, the blood of the innocent, clashed like an explosive charge against Lucifer's, fusing it permanently into the singed edges of the blade.

Stunned, Lucifer staggered back into the wall of wheat, his wide, angry eyes riveted on the weapon in my hands. I could see in his eyes that he had never expected this and I felt shocked myself. In all of time, there had never been a physical confrontation among angels, let alone archangels.

"You strike your own brother?" he barked, "And for what?" The last question was a genuine search for an answer to what he could not comprehend. His eyes were, once again, sharp and cold as he stared at me and waited for a response.

At that moment, although I felt that I was justified in what I had done, I also felt remorseful, but my young pride would never allow me to admit it. "For justice. As obedience to Father and punishment for what you've done to Man," I said, looking down at the marked blade, its edge now a dark red. "From now on, I will carry this scythe as a symbol so that I can always remember why Man strayed from the path of God." And as I looked ahead, my eyes locked with Lucifer's, and an understanding dawned between us. We had become adversaries in a never ending war in which only battles would be won. "You and I are no longer brothers," I said, "but as day and night are bound by a common horizon, we are linked to one another by a common line, the soul of Man. From now on, I will do anything that I can to shield Man from you, and even if you do succeed to deceive him I will be there to offer redemption to every parting soul." Unforeseen by me, the oath that I took at that moment changed my essence and completed my transformation. My wings, already jet black, reflected the darkness that surrounded and challenged me at every moment thereafter, and I discarded white and chose black as my disguise; maybe as a compliment to my new companion, the *crow*. I named it Bran.

There was an intense moment of silence, and I believe that we both felt the rip of our brotherhood. A sadness washed over me, dampening my anger, and I felt the weight of the loss on my soul, and I saw, ever so briefly, the same cloud pass over Lucifer. But before I could say anything, Lucifer's countenance changed and he returned my look with an amused smile. "An eternal battle for Man's soul?" he mused. "Be careful what you commit to, brother, for tomorrow things never feel as they do today. You don't understand the burden that you just accepted."

Lucifer's comment was not an opinion, but a statement of fact in his usual and arrogant way. For him, it was the end of our conversation. At that instant, the slashed flesh on his forearm glowed red as the separated skin fused, leaving behind a cicatrice. Lucifer looked down at his arm and nodded. We both knew that this would be the first of many scars. He turned and as he was leaving said, "I will leave you now to care for young Abel. I think that Cain will be presently wandering my way and I need to show him the path he has chosen. How fitting that we both receive our first soul on the same day." And as he disappeared, "Eternity begins today."

I brought the scythe down to my side and stared at the spot where Lucifer had last stood. I was not sorry for what I had said or done, for ultimately, it had to be and I had known it for some time. All I could do was lament what was to come, although I had no idea as to its magnitude. Brothers as we were, we were walking opposite paths with the human soul as the median. I shrugged off the emotions and walked to Abel's limp body and knelt down. I knew what I had to do for Abel's soul, but had no idea how to handle the rest. So, I let my instincts take over. Reverently, I held his face in my hands and with his lips inches away breathed into his mouth. A misty, diaphanous cloud swirled between us as Abel's soul was retrieved into mine, its temporary vessel. It was momentous, the redemption of the first soul, and I was completely consumed by its presence. Through it, I felt the uplifting feeling of absolute freedom and was touched by the nobility of its essence. At that moment, there was no doubt as to the validity of my decision. Time and existence, however, have a way of clouding things.

EIGHT

Sometimes, when I think back to Cain and Abel, I recall how lost and frustrated I felt that day. Something precious had been violently taken from humanity and I wanted, needed, all of creation to partake in delivering justice. But I soon learned that I was alone in this fight – as I had to be, and as humanity continued down its path of selfishness and destruction, I grew numb in my role as the savior of the soul. I learned how to use shadows, darkness, fire, thunder and lightning to instill fear in Man's heart when wickedness was rampant, and offer redemption simply as a means to get back at Lucifer. For thousands of years, that was the way, but then, for a brief moment, I was touched by the light and once again believed in Man, just to have it savagely torn from me. This time, however, the pain was too unbearable and what I did today cannot be undone.

The day of Abel's death, the first murder, continued as bright and sunny as nature had intended. The darkness was in me as I hunted down my first prey.

From above, I saw a young man with an uncanny resemblance to Abel. He walked quickly along the dirt road heading for the cluster of caves at the base of Mount Qasioun. His pace was brisk and his body movements tense as he nervously pushed his dark hair repeatedly away from his forehead with trembling fingers.

I moved in for the kill and crash landed on the path in front of him. The ferocity of my assault shook the earth and sent dirt, rubble and stone in every direction. The young man stumbled awkwardly and screeched in pain as shattered shards of stone randomly cut into his body. But just as abruptly, everything was once again calm and quiet. He stood where he was, squinting through the settling dust, his eyes riveted on the not so angelic figure that was me – demonic would come later. I was crouched on one knee and blocking the path ahead of him. I looked up and the man gasped, but not because he had realized who I was. His eyes had fallen on the scythe – his scythe – which I held tightly in my right hand, its handle resting on the ground like a flagpole with its blade towering above me. Gently, Bran landed on my shoulder and cawed.

I remained motionless, my muscles tight and ready to spring. I did not want to act rashly, but it was difficult, and when I spoke it was in a guttural and almost animalistic whisper. "Cain, *where* is Abel?"

Cain eyed the scythe nervously, but I could see that the initial panic that he felt was subsiding. He knew that I, as an archangel, was there to serve Man and could not harm him. "I don't know. I'm not his babysitter," he said curtly, even arrogantly, as he shifted his position and took a step closer to me, forcing me to have to look up at him if I wanted to meet his eyes. But I did not flinch or move a muscle and stared ahead at nothing.

"Do you see the blade in front of you? It's covered with your brother's innocent blood," I said. "Be humble and repent while I'm still willing to offer you such mercy. But I want you to know," I continued, still on my knees, "if it was not for Father, I would do to you with this same blade what you did to Abel, but tenfold." And then, without warning, looking up or moving anything but my arm, I swung the scythe through the air and brought it down with great force to within inches of his face. "Is this not your scythe?"

Cain choked a squeamish cry and stared at the blood-charred blade barely touching his forehead. "You know it is, so why the games? Abel is dead and nothing can change that," he blurted, taking a short breath and momentarily closing his eyes to recompose as I rested the scythe once again at my side and slowly got to my feet. Cain's face was still pale but when he continued, his tone was controlled and demanding, "Tell me what will happen to me." It was obvious that he wasn't sorry for what he had done. "You can't do anything to me!" he said, but then added as an afterthought, "But if the people find out what I've done, they will kill me. You have to protect me!"

I stared at Cain and tried to be angelic or compassionate; after all, he was Adam's son. But there was nothing in me but contempt. I wanted him to suffer. "Yes, they will. And no, I don't," was my icy response. But then, I had an idea. Maybe if I managed to deny Lucifer his first condemned soul, humanity could still be saved from the forces of temptation and darkness that he had cast on it. Yes, I know. I was naïve and didn't know what the *man* in *human* was truly capable of and the depths he would willingly submerge to for power and fame. The glory of immortality, what a damning illusion. Pointing to Cain, I said, "You will die and I can let Lucifer have you. You'd be the first condemned soul." The fear in his eyes at that instant gave me great satisfaction, just as it did today; different eyes, different killer, same damned soul.

Cain watched with alarm and took a step backwards as I passed the scythe from my right to my left hand, but the movement was casual and it became obvious that I wasn't going to use it as a weapon against him. Instead, I closed my right hand and pointed to his chest. Almost immediately, my finger ignited in blue flames. I grinned.

"What are you –" Cain started to ask, but the answer became apparent and he bellowed a primeval roar of pain. He looked down and what he saw horrified him. The tan skin to the left of his chest was scaring with red tissue as it burned. Cain screamed in agony, his terrified gaze passing between his chest and me repeatedly. "You can't do this!" he screamed.

I wasn't quite sure if I could or not, but it didn't matter. The rules of the game had changed, and I had to adapt. Lucifer would not get his soul; at least not on that day. "I think you're mistaken," I said in a tranquil voice, "because, well, I'm doing it and who's to stop me?" Cain screamed while I continued. But what I was doing was not a banal form of torture or punishment. It was a branding and it had a very significant purpose in my mind; to mark ownership of that soul. Slowly, the scarred tissue began to take shape and defined a snake in the form of the number six. It was Man's number in Lucifer's image, the serpent of Eden. I extinguished the flame and released Cain from my hold. He fell to his knees and whimpered like a wronged dog. The mark was finished and permanently set. I looked down at him and all I saw was a deplorable being void of any dignity. This duality, the nobility that I had felt through Abel and the debasement of Man's soul through Cain, would become the bane of my existence.

"As of today, you will be known to all for the evil that you are by the mark that you bear. And you will wander the earth for as long as there is lust and desire in your heart. No one will dare touch you in fear of my retaliation." I stopped and stared at the mark. It was the first one and stayed like that for thousands of years. Until today, when I inflicted it again on another soul just as wicked. I blinked and the room was dark again, the robed figure motionless where I had last seen her.

NINE

Her restraint was slowly getting under my skin. How could she sit there and listen without comment or emotion? Weren't women supposed to be all emotional and compassionate when it comes to injustice and other people's pain? Apparently not. She was, most certainly, a better man than I. I shrugged and decided to continue. What difference did it make what she thought? Recounting my story was liberating and I wanted to tell it, get it all out in the open and let her know why we were where we were. I turned and looked at the single candlestick at the far end of the table. It was almost completely burned out, its orange light flickering hopelessly as it tried to fend off the invading darkness. Suddenly, the light became blindingly bright and I had to close my eyes. When I opened them again, just seconds later, I was there no more, but standing in the Room of Candles. The carved wood doors were open and I could feel the gentle breeze that nourished the never ending rows of hundreds of thousands of tiny burning lights. Michael was there, leaning against the doorframe while intently watching my every move, and behind him, almost swallowed by the dark, I could make out the silhouette of the hooded figure.

It was rare for Michael to visit me. It usually meant that I had done something of which he did not approve, or that in his mind I needed counseling – if I had known how profitable that profession would become, I wouldn't have accepted this one. I shrugged it off and walked back and forth between the rows of lights and extinguished candles here and there with the tip of my finger, my pace deliberate and unconcerned. To the common observer, my countenance and demeanor were relaxed and without intention, but Michael was my brother, the one closest to me, and I knew that he could feel the charged energy caged beneath my seemingly callous and uninterested demeanor. I stopped in front of a bronze plate hanging on the wall at the end of one of the rows and looked at my reflection. I looked older and more mature – or maybe just tired and spent, but the lines on my face were real and they attested to the thousands of years that I served humanity since the murder of Abel. This servitude had its toll on me, and although I tried hard to maintain my beliefs, I was not the same altruistic young angel who for five millennia stood up to Lucifer as a shield for Man and showed love and empathy for all souls; well, almost all. The monstrosity of human history – rampant with war and destruction, chipped away at me relentlessly and I felt disillusioned and empty. I needed a break from it all – the barbaric ways of Man; doesn't matter what they called themselves: Goths, Vandals, Vikings, Celts, Mongols, Huns, Spartans, Nazis; I could go on and on because humanity simply doesn't stop – and although I didn't know it then, that break would soon come and knock me off of my feet. Funny thing, it's never how you imagine it or would like it to be.

"You know, Michael, each one of these candles represents a human soul and with each one that I put out I'm ending a life." I stopped walking and looked down at the row of candles on the wooden sill before me, and as I located the one I was looking for, a dim recollection of how unnerving the notion of death had once been nudged at me. I shrugged off the feeling and smothered the light without the least bit of hesitation. "There goes another, just like that," I said, and snapped my fingers in a gesture that showed the simplicity of what I had done. "All sorts of people: pedophile priests, corrupt kings, beggars, alcoholics, drug dealers, thieves, murderers, prostitutes… you name it, I got it. This one, for example," I said, and pointed to the candle that I had just extinguished, "was a heartless tyrant. Can you imagine that? Causing the murder and death of thousands and then being offered a chance at redemption? Not today, I'm too dangerous. It's just safer for everyone for me to come here and take care of business with the tip of my finger."

I glanced at Michael, but Michael looked on without comment or expression. He knew me too well, and although I knew he wanted to talk and counsel me, he was not going to engage in any sort of discussion with me; not now. Instead, he was going to patiently listen and wait the storm out as I paced around my stone-walled cage and vented until I had nothing left. Then, he would do what he usually does; try and make me *see*. But I had other plans. I wanted a discussion, a confrontation, and I was going to get it. I lifted my index finger and for a moment held it deliberately over a burning flame. Then, slowly, I brought it down on the wick of the candle and snuffed it out. "Oops," I gasped, and looked at Michael with alarm.

The significance of what had just happened made Michael jump from the doorframe in horror. He stared at me in disbelief, eyes and mouth open wide in shock at the thought of an innocent life having mistakenly been taken, and so carelessly. I chuckled and half smiled to myself; it was a mean thing to do, but now I had him.

"Sorry, bad joke. Her time was up," I said with a look of abandon, and walked to the end of the row and faced Michael. "So, Michael, commander of the army of God, the patron saint of chivalry, the one who will make the earth tremble and show man what it is to fear God. What is it that I've done this time? What do you want from me?"

Michael quickly regained his composure and took advantage of my momentarily resigned demeanor. He placed his hand on my shoulder and said, "That may be so, and yet, it's not me who is the bearer of the choice for eternal life or damnation." There was a pause, as he stopped to look at me. "Azrail, I'm worried about you and what you do."

I didn't reply immediately but managed a grin, and although I had heard this before, many times, I still appreciated my brother's concern. These conversations, however, tended towards discussions and misunderstandings. "Don't worry yourself, I'm fine," I said calmly with a smile. "As for you," I added with a grin, "I can personally guarantee that there are no plans for taking your life… yet." I finished with a wide smile.

It was a good joke and it felt good to talk freely and without concern for a change. I looked at Michael, hoping to see a smirk or a laugh, but Michael was Michael, and when he had something on his mind, nothing could distract him or change his mood. Not even a good joke.

"You know that's not what I meant," Michael retorted, probably a bit harsher than he intended. Then, in a milder, almost remorseful tone, he said, "You've changed through the centuries. The Azrail I see today is far from the archangel he set out to be. And though you cannot see it, the arrogance and contempt that you show for human life will someday be the weapons Lucifer will use to destroy you." Michael stopped briefly and looked around the room at the thousands of candles. "You play with Man's soul as if it's all a joke."

I knew what Michael said was true, but knowing and accepting are not complementary, and it was exactly what I resented and hated about myself. Through the ages, I had become more and more like Lucifer and viewed Man with cynicism. But be that as it may, I would never admit it and words alone could never heal the scars. I took a step back, forcing Michael's hand off my shoulder. "It's not a joke. I have yet to see a single Man smile when they see me coming," I said icily. "In the end, I get the job done and do what I have to do; *my way!*" The last two words were said harshly through gritted teeth with no sign of resignation. "And yes, I always do my best to thwart Lucifer in any way that I can, but there are just some souls that do not deserve a second chance. He can take those and keep them company."

Michael looked at me, and although he was always honest and to the point – most of the time brutally so – the change that I noticed in him was quite subtle, almost indiscernible. Your eyes never fail to give you away, and I was now looking into a pair that were gentler and more understanding. "Azrail, your courage and strength have always been remarkable and an example for us, but you have become blind to yourself. Please, listen to what I'm saying." Michael took a step forward, his hands held out in a gesture of truce. "You cannot disobey Father and not suffer the consequences. Letting your emotions or personal agenda interfere with your duties is not permissible. Every soul deserves deliverance; you *know* that!"

No shit! Of course I knew that, it was the basis of my existence. And who the hell could defy Father and get away with it, anyway? Wasn't Lucifer the ultimate example? But for him to say it was irritating and simply added to my feelings of self-pity; the world's lack of understanding of what I had already endured and what was yet to come. My response was a statement of defiance. It was instinctive and driven by a primal need for self-preservation. "And what do you know about what I do? Are you mad? I do what I have to do to shield the little sanity or empathy that I still have! Now, how I do it is my business and neither you nor anyone else has a say in it," I shouted. "As I recall, while you and Gabriel cowered from Mother

Earth and even tried to stop me, I dove in head first – literally, and almost burned to cinders in the process, but never gave up, and lo and behold managed to bring what Father had asked for." I paused, but before Michael could answer, continued in a derisive tone, "You see, Michael, I have power and that's something you can never understand. So don't lecture me about what's right and wrong, because while you sit around waiting to save or defend humanity, I'm knee deep in human shit. Now, leave me be!"

"Azrail, please listen," pleaded Michael, "because of your arrogance Father will test you and that's all that Lucifer wants. You know he will pounce on the opportunity to destroy you, don't give him the satisfaction."

It's damning how we can look back at specific moments in time and see how wrong we were. This was one of those defining moments. But I was bitter and frustrated and believed myself superior to Lucifer, and if at that instant I resented being the keeper of man's soul, it was nothing when compared to the ingrown enmity that had established itself between myself and Lucifer. "Let him come," I said. The conversation was over; I turned and walked away.

TEN

Time has no essence or meaning for me, so it doesn't heal anything. Different than for Man, everything is always present; all of creation and its history. Nothing ever fades. So, each encounter with Lucifer only helped escalate the infected and festering wound that was our contemptuous relationship. But what happened next, the sheer dimension of it, destroyed the small illusion of hope that I still had for Man, and made me believe that Father himself had given up. At least, that's how I saw it; but I was wrong. If Man chose to cave into his selfish desires and willingly accept what Lucifer had to offer, then he had to be punished, but not discarded. I couldn't see that, because for me it was no longer about Man's soul and redemption. The only thing I saw, the only reason behind any effort that I exerted in saving Man, was my rivalry with Lucifer and the chore at hand was a great blow to my efforts.

The ancient city of Hebron – named after Abraham, was clearly visible from where we – Michael, Gabriel and I, stood on the mountain side to its west, with the twin cities of Sodom and Gomorrah hidden behind the hills to the south. It was a rocky hillside, studded with young and old olive trees, and the aroma of desert migwort was pleasant. I heard a caw and looked over to my right to find my loyal companion perched on a knotty and withered olive branch. Its twisted and gnarled trunk was old, almost as old as life, and I wondered how much longer it would still be there. Would righteousness ever completely cease to exist? I thought of my mission and grinned wryly. It was time to find out. I looked down at the small plain of Mamre below and pointed to a man sitting under a tent pitched under the shade of a grove of oak trees beside a stream. Michael and Gabriel nodded and we started down the path, the heat on our backs merciless despite the cool midafternoon breeze.

Abraham was sitting on a simple chair by his tent door and resting his bare feet on the beautifully ornate rug that was placed there for him. His sandals were on the ground beside the rug, and as was tradition, he had already washed his hands and feet in preparation for supper. He took a sip from a glass of sugar and vinegar sherbet and slowly savored it before swallowing. The day had been long and arduous, but as he sat there and looked at the sheep grazing in the field in front of him, his heart was filled with satisfaction. Little did he know about the message that we were about to bring him. That's the beauty of not knowing, or the lover not seeing.

The sun was setting when we reached the fields below the mountain and made it difficult for Abraham to look in our direction without having to squint. All that he could make out was the silhouette of three men walking down the path toward his camp. But that didn't impede his correct judgment of us. The lack of horses or any baggage made it obvious that we were not travelers, and that we were there to meet him. It was not the customary time of the day for receiving company, but nevertheless, Abraham did not mind the idea of pleasant companionship and news from Hebron. He turned his head to the tent looking for his wife, Sarah, but she was not there. To his surprise, when he looked back we were standing in front of him. Abraham jumped to his feet and momentarily looked dumfounded, but then immediately kneeled and bowed his head.

"My Lord, if I have found favor in your sight, pass not by without rest and food, I pray you," he said.

I glanced at Gabriel – who was the one most likely to accept the offer, and shook my head, then turned my attention back to Abraham who was still on his knees and looking at the ground. Father had once again burdened me with the task of punishing humanity, and I felt harried and distraught. Actually, I was pissed and didn't understand why we had to visit Abraham at all, let alone waste time with pleasantries. I knew what was coming. I would destroy the cities of Sodom and Gomorrah and then face Lucifer and listen to him gloat about being right; there was no way out, humanity had screwed me again. I opened my mouth to answer, but before I could say anything, Gabriel responded.

"My brother, Abraham, cease your obeisance. We shall do as you please," said Gabriel, touching Abraham's shoulder.

I took a deep breath and turned to Gabriel. There were no need for words, for my despondent stare said it all. Abraham stood and looked at us one by one, stopping on me. All in black, scythe in hand, long hair, stubble and a bad temper; I was indeed a frightful sight befitting the incongruent image that people had created of me. His eyes were kind but sharp, and I felt them searching mine for hints as to the tenor of our visit. It was obvious that we were there to talk to him, but about what he could not start to imagine. I wonder if he would have been as patient if he knew I had come to destroy his people. Or maybe he knew, because I could see the sadness in his smile.

"Let a little water be fetched to wash the dust from your feet and hands, and rest yourselves under the shade of the oak," he said as he motioned towards the trees by the stream. "And I will fetch a morsel of food to comfort your hearts before you tell me what it is that you seek." With this, he turned and headed for the tent.

Almost immediately, Hagar, a young Egyptian maiden wearing a white gown with red details on the waist and shoulders and carrying a large bundle of cloth under her arm, came from the tent and walked past us to a shaded spot by the stream. Her skin was fair and her hair, black as the night, fell loosely over her shoulders. She did not look at us even once, but immediately put the bundle on the ground and quickly cleared the stones and fallen branches from the area under the oak. She then unfolded the bundle and spread a flowery cloth on the ground. On it, she placed beautifully woven pillows and several ornate bowls with nuts and dried fruit before returning to the tent.

Our meal wasn't a king's feast, but I have to admit that it was delicious and helped calm me down and slightly dampen my feelings of anger and frustration. Sarah, Abraham's wife, prepared fresh bread on the hearth – which we ate with cheese, herbs and milk, while Abraham had one of the servants prepare a young calf over the fire. I ate quietly and kept to myself, hoping to find an opportune moment to tell Abraham why we were there. Sarah's presence, however, made that impossible. Michael, as usual, more interested in food and not much of a talker, ate like there was no tomorrow. So, Gabriel – with his well-mannered ways, was left with the task of engaging in cordial conversation. The small talk went on for over an hour when, finally, with the sky glowing red and the sun beginning to set behind the hills, we were ready to address the true purpose of our visit. We got up and started to walk at a leisurely pace toward the hill opposite from where we had come. I still wasn't listening and was lost in my own thoughts about the inevitable encounter with Lucifer when Gabriel stopped walking and turned back to face Sarah and Hagar. They were busy clearing the dishes and what was left of the food, but stopped when they noticed Gabriel looking at them.

Addressing Sarah in a low and reflective tone, Gabriel said, "My dear woman, I will return to these lands in the future and see you with son."

I was surprised by Gabriel's comment, but it was obvious that Sarah was even more so. She stood there momentarily transfixed with wide, open eyes and then, regaining herself, giggled with amusement and responded, "Surely not, my Lord. I am aged and had not the pleasure even in youth. How can it be now, with my lord being old also?"

"Why do you laugh? Do you doubt your Lord?" asked Gabriel. "Is anything too hard for the Lord?" he affirmed, and as he turned to leave, continued, "I will return to these lands and surely see you with son."

Abraham hesitantly, apprehensively looked at Gabriel. I could tell that he was worried that Gabriel might be offended by Sarah's remark, but he didn't know Gabriel. Gabriel's calm and unperturbed manner, however, made him relax and once again we resumed our walk up the path to the hill that led to the cities of Sodom and Gomorrah. It was an easy and pleasurable walk, but I had already lost my somewhat relaxed after-dinner state and felt anxious to get things going. I wanted to dive headfirst into the storm and didn't care much about the consequences, so I hastened my pace and forced everyone to keep up with me. I only stopped when we reached the top of the hill and turned to find only Abraham and Gabriel close behind me. Michael, being Michael, had slowed his pace and stayed behind, not wanting to get involved. He was content with his role as warrior guardian, and this meeting was more about diplomacy. I was the executioner who had his orders and had to get things done, while Gabriel was there for damage control and to negotiate the terms of the contract before the inevitable slap. But you see, there *was* no negotiation this time, just the courtesy of information and the slap would be more like a kick in the crotch. I nodded for Gabriel to start.

Gabriel looked at Abraham, smiled and said in a caring tone, "Great prophet Abraham, commander and shepherd of your people, Father has sent us forth to investigate the cry of grievous sin that reaches the heavens from the cities of Sodom and Gomorrah, and it wouldn't be proper to hide from you that which must be done."

Abraham didn't respond immediately or show any signs of surprise, instead he stroked his beard in thought. I could tell that he knew what we were there for, after all, it wasn't the first time that Man had to be punished. What worried him was not the result of the investigation, but rather the actions that would be taken as rectification. "And if it is true? And if Sodom and Gomorrah are truly cities of sin, what will my Lord do?"

Gabriel put his hand on Abraham's shoulder and smiled, his eyes betraying the sorrow that he felt in his heart, and replied, "Dear Abraham, Father would never do anything that He would deem as unjust. Everything that He does is for the good of Man."

Abraham bowed in acknowledgment, but his concern and love for his people did not allow him to concede just yet. "Yes, of course. But my Lord, I must know what you will do? Surely, not another flood?"

Gabriel sighed. "No, not a flood. But for Father to create, he must first destroy."

"But how? I do not understand."

It was one thing to be courteous, or as Gabriel put it, diplomatic, and inform the prophet of our mission, but this was getting us nowhere so I stepped forward with a loud, "Stop!" Both men turned to me simultaneously as I continued, "We're going to invite everyone and have a barbeque, of course. And, oh yes, I almost forgot; we're also going to burn the cities to the ground and end the Godlessness and promiscuity." Then, in a more serious tone, "Father wants you to come with us and witness His wrath so that you can recount it for generations to come, and let Man know what happens when he disobeys God's will. Fear *always* supersedes love when obedience is concerned."

Abraham looked baffled, and for the first time I realized that maybe he was not quite onboard with us. I guess too much diplomacy and useless repartee had clouded the message, but isn't that the rule of politics; eat, mingle, talk and screw around but never say anything concrete? I smirked. Abraham, still unsure of what I meant, turned from me to Gabriel and said, "Forgive me, my Lord, but how will burning the cities to the ground end Godlessness and sin? It does not make sense. Wickedness and promiscuity have infested Man and must be purged from the soul. The people of these towns need to be cleansed of their sins, not turned into homeless beggars."

Gabriel exhaled and lowered his gaze. It's never easy to look someone in the eye and tell them a truth that you know will hurt them.

"I'm afraid you didn't understand, Abraham. The people will burn with the cities."

Abraham stumbled backward and would have fallen if I hadn't grabbed him by the arm. It was clear that although he expected some kind of punishment, this was far more drastic than what he had imagined. "Our Father in heaven, this cannot be. What about the faithful? Will you also destroy the righteous with the wicked?" Abraham paused and stared at Gabriel, not daring to blink.

Gabriel knew the truth, we all did, so the response wasn't difficult or compromising, "If there are righteous people in the city, then we will spare them and the cities."

I thought the answer was quite clear; righteous people... spared city! But Abraham wasn't convinced, or wasn't willing to accept the fact that there was no hope. "What if there are only fifty?" he asked.

"The cities shall be spared."

"And twenty?" continued Abraham.

"Assuredly, Father will spare the cities," responded Gabriel, patiently.

I moved a couple of steps away from them and glanced at Michael. Michael looked at me and shrugged; this was Gabriel's territory. But I wasn't quite sure that Gabriel had it in him to deliver the final blow. He was stalling, going along with this pointless banter knowing well that I had been against it the whole time. The delay was making me impatient, and nothing good ever came from me losing my patience. I ran my fingers through my hair and glanced at Abraham.

"And ten?"

Goddamn it – exactly what we were there for, the damning of souls – was he going to countdown one by one to zero? "Enough!" I cut in, "If you really have to know, I will burn everything and everyone. If Father ordained it, then there *are* no righteous men, not even one." I caught Gabriel's alarmed look, but was past the point to care. "But tell you what, if there happen to be a few deserving wretches among these infidels, I will expel them so they can die in the desert heat. Satisfied?"

Even Michael was stunned by my outburst and quickly walked up to my side. He gently but firmly put his hand on my shoulder.

"Azrail, have you lost your mind? This is Abraham that you're talking to." Gabriel's admonition was calm but strict.

I placed my thumb and forefinger over my eyes and slowly pinched the bridge of my nose. As my hand moved down my face I felt the week-old stubble on my cheeks and neck; what the hell was I doing? I think I was the first bipolar angel. "I beg your forgiveness, Abraham, but my responsibilities towards humanity have caused me great sorrow and distress. I don't understand how Man can so readily forget his bounty and break the laws that even animals don't dare break." I paused, but not because I expected an answer. There was no answer to be given. *Tempt man long enough and he will sin*; Lucifer's motto – but he did much more than come up with a catchy slogan, he was there, always there, and ready at every turn to make sure it would happen. I felt a new wave of revolt and quiet frustration engulf me. "And yet, here I am once again about to make an example of Man for misguided and uncontrolled use of free will – carrying the burden of these condemned souls while Lucifer, my dear brother Lucifer, sits back and receives the spoils." I stopped and stared at the cities of Sodom and Gomorrah glowing in the night horizon and shouted, "Thousands handed to him on a silver platter by *me*!"

Abraham was not shocked or upset by my outburst. To the contrary, he simply looked at me and I could see the kindness in his eyes. "Then, I will accompany you and aid you with this unbearable task."

I didn't know how to react to that kindness. Empathy and altruism had been shoved deep into the recesses of my being while I was completely consumed in a battle between myself and Lucifer; but ever so more with myself. "Oh, but you misunderstand. I feel no remorse in taking the lives of the wretched. It's Lucifer receiving their souls that revolts me."

Abraham lowered his gaze and turned away. He stood humbly with his hands folded in front of him lost in his own thoughts. To my eyes, he suddenly looked much older, much more feeble. Gabriel hesitated, but then took a few steps in his direction, stopping just short of his back. In a quiet voice, almost as if he didn't want to be heard at all, he said, "Sorry, Abraham, but it may be best that you not accompany us. But, rest assured that we will take care of your nephew, Lot, and his family."

I looked at Gabriel in disgust and rolled my eyes. Damn, why did Gabriel always have to complicate things? Abraham didn't ask for anything! All we – actually I, had to do was destroy the cities and get out. But no, that wasn't enough. Because now, I also had to offer my babysitting services to Lot and his family. As I was about to object, it hit me. This was a good thing.

ELEVEN

The sun had gone down and the sky was a deep blue with hundreds of brilliant stars swimming in its vastness. It was almost a heavenly sight, if not for one particularly bright, red star singled out like a hermit above the cities of Sodom and Gomorrah. Gabriel and I were standing in front of the main gate, staring at the stone walls that loomed high above us. I remember thinking, although quite a barrier for men, how idiotic they were for us. The gate was massive, made of solid oak and bolted with iron. Above it, positioned in the center of the supporting arc and protruding outward, was a large stone, phallic sculpture. Below it was written: *Here Lives Happiness.* I noticed that Gabriel looked away embarrassed, but his unamused look told me that if there was any doubt in his mind before, there was none now. I looked up at the lonely star and wondered how long after giving the signal Michael would start the assault, and how long before it was all over.

We walked through the gate without a word and proceeded down a well-lit street that almost immediately opened into a wide, mostly empty, inner court. Houses, shops and small buildings surrounded it, their continuity only broken by a few narrow streets that led away to the inner city and the dwellings beyond. I was quite surprised at the cleanliness and charm of the whole place and for an instant wanted to believe that we were mistaken; that's when I saw it. Smack in the middle of the courtyard, a lavishly promiscuous fountain was making an unmistakable statement. The outside wall of the pool was covered with colorful square tiles, individually hand painted and portraying a myriad of sexual acts, while the main sculpture, made of marble, characterized a Herculean figure with a disproportionately large and erect organ shooting water into the pool below. I quickly glanced at Gabriel, but he had turned his back to the fountain and was looking around in disbelief. I followed his gaze and realized what we had walked into – the red lights were on and Roxanne was hard at work. There were men wearing nothing but loincloths and women in loose, flowing and semi-transparent gowns with nothing underneath standing in the shadows and doorways, who when approached by others – men, women or both – disappeared into the buildings behind them.

In the past, I had chastised Man for all sorts of transgressions. In the beginning it had been difficult witnessing the depths of darkness to which humanity could plummet, but as it is with everything, past scars worked like a shield and made me more and more callous; just like a child who becomes insensitive to punishment, I had become indifferent to the immoralities of humanity. But this time it was different. I felt embarrassed that Gabriel was there; and protective. *I* was used to it, but seeing the shock and aversion on Gabriel's face made me want to lash out and destroy indiscriminately; I had to prevent the scarring, I would not allow him to go down the same path as I. If I had to punish Man while protecting it from Lucifer, then so be it, but Gabriel had to stand beside Man and protect him from himself. Without thought about the promise we had made to Abraham, I looked up and was about to give the signal when, suddenly, a man hastily entered the court from the street closest to us. I stopped to look at him as he stood there gasping for air. He was obviously a wealthy man, wearing a purple undergarment of fine linen bound by a girdle, a colorful vesture, a head cloth, and leather sandals. He quickly glanced around the yard and, although quite out of breath, promptly headed toward us. As he reached Gabriel, who was a foot or two ahead of me, he bowed low and said, "My Lord, uncle sent word that you would be arriving tonight. Your presence here is an honor and a privilege." The man stopped, took a breath and then continued, "Please allow me to offer you a place to eat and rest before you continue on your journey." He paused, and although he was bent with his eyes cast downward, I could see him furtively look from door to door and absorb everything that he already knew was taking place in every dark corner. In an embarrassed but urgent tone, he said, "We should leave, my Lord. It's not appropriate to be outside after dark. People may misunderstand."

I didn't worry about Gabriel's answer, his look of discomfort said it all, but I did wonder about Abraham's sincerity since it was obvious that he had warned Lot even before our visit to him. I shrugged it off and turned to face the colossal limb that so defined that Trojan monument. To my surprise, and I'm not sure why it surprised me anymore, my calling card was already there impatiently hopping from side to side on the offensive structure. It was a confirmation. I had an important – and I'm not embarrassed to say – somewhat enjoyable task at hand. I winked at Bran, and it cawed and jumped up to watch from the statue's head.

Gabriel looked down at the man and said, "You must be Lot, Abraham's nephew. We weren't expecting to see you so soon." He motioned for Lot to stand. "We thank you for your generosity, but I think that we will spend the night in town and get to know the people and their ways. From what I see, it's quite evident that we will have business to tend to for Father before the night is done; and not a pleasant affair at that."

Lot straightened, but still couldn't bring himself to look at Gabriel. "Please, my Lord, come spend the evening at my house with my family. We are not wealthy, but my wife has prepared a delightful meal. You may even see things differently after some food and rest?"

I was only half listening to Lot's lugubrious drivel as I stretched out my arm to the night sky and summoned the powers that were natural only to me. There was a deafening clap of thunder, the first of many on that ominous night, and I felt myself instantly energized. I can't lie, because the thought of it even today – the power that I possessed, makes me grin. My outstretched arm erupted with raw energy and I reveled at the sight of my hand and fingers engulfed in that maze of electricity. Blinding, blue bolts jumped from the tips of my fingers as my scythe materialized in my grip. Without hesitation, I lifted it above my head and brought it forcefully down on the fountain's outstretched phallus. The sound of metal crashing against stone was earsplitting as bits and pieces of the Herculean penis exploded in every direction. The godly but yet offensive fountain figure had been castrated. I looked at Gabriel and grinned at his surprised but agreeable smile. As for Lot, his horrified look and constantly darting eyes said it all.

"Very good, *now* we can go to your house. I'm hungry, the town can wait," I said, and started to walk in the direction Lot had come from. Bran cawed and took off into the night.

I'm not sure to what extent people knew what was coming, but I'm sure that their anxiety was heightened, for although they wanted to rush out and see what all the commotion was about, my presence – and, oh, I'm pretty sure they knew that I wasn't just any man, made them stay inside and peer from behind curtains or cracked doors. But as soon as we were gone, naked bodies ran into the street and stared and gasped at what was left of their symbol of virility. One, however, cloaked and unrecognizable, sneaked out of one of the houses and followed us. I felt his presence, but why would I care? That, maybe, was a mistake.

TWELVE

Lot's house was nothing close to being modest. Everything was bright and vibrant, from the tapestries on the walls to the colorful drapes on the windows. Even the stone floors were covered with expensive, silk rugs. Everything was a show of state and dignity rather than for ordinary use. It made me want to call Bran and have him hop around and peck at things just to leave his mark and make things look a bit used. But alas, we were guests and I had to temporarily behave. It would all soon be gone anyway.

I stood in the middle of the living room and pondered where to sit. Gabriel had graciously accepted Lot's offer and was sitting on a masterfully hand-decorated, plush chair. I couldn't find another like it and everything else looked too delicate, so I finally chose a wooden chair that seemed strong enough to hold my weight and sat down. It was hand carved with exceptional details and although I wasn't one to notice or care about these things, the carvings of the intertwining branches around godly figures were impressive. To my dismay, however, it was butt bruisingly uncomfortable. Obviously, the maker – or owner, for that matter, was more concerned with looks and status rather than the comfort it should offer the poor bastard sitting on it. I looked around for some pillows, but didn't see any. I shook my head at the display of so much useless wealth, and wondered how many camel loads it had taken. I knew that Abraham and Lot returned from Egypt very rich men, but Lot – quite unlike his uncle, had made sure to let his fellow Man know. Why was putting oneself above others so important to Man? What the hell did status mean once you were in my crosshairs? Then, I noticed some decorative, silk pillows laying on the dresser-cabinet-chest thingy by the wall next to me. I reached over and grabbed a few. They felt soft and expensive, most definitely bordering on insulting. I grinned and stood. Unceremoniously, I threw some on the seat under me and shoved a couple of them behind my back as I sat back down.

I thought of my place, the Room of Candles, with its thousands of burning lights and felt a chill run through my spine; it was nothing but bare, stone walls, floors and wood. Ironically, I remember thinking how a woman would make that room – what is the center of life and death, so much more agreeable. But then again, it might look like this, and the colors simply hurt my eyes and the amount of inutile junk numbed my brain. I also didn't care for pleasantries or have time for company, so its bareness suited me perfectly. The truth of it was that Man was proud, competitive, and greedy, and the measure of his wealth was his home and how many sheep he owned. Admittedly, owning sheep had its many advantages among men, but I wasn't Man. I did, however, know an egotistical, offensive goat!

The meal, like the house, was also way overboard. But that, I didn't mind. There was plenty of everything and it was all lavishly prepared by Lot's wife. The fact that it was ready when we arrived, however, made me wary once more. Not that it mattered much, since there was no way that anyone, not even Abraham, could hide what was going on in the city. But the fact that Lot knew we were coming made me uncomfortable and my thoughts automatically centered on Lucifer and his conniving nature. The freshly baked bread, tender lamb meat with mint, and plenty of red wine, however, soon made me forget my worries and relax.

Unfortunately, our respite did not last very long. As Lot's wife and two daughters cleared the silver dishes and what remained of the food, a distant and unnatural rumbling filled the air. Lot jumped to his feet and, without uttering a single word, ran to the courtyard. I lazily motioned for Gabriel to get up and we followed. Once outside, we saw a mob of men approaching the house. I couldn't tell, but it looked like, apart from torches, they were also carrying makeshift weapons; some rakes, shovels and clubs. Gabriel looked at me and I saw that he was concerned. I shrugged and smiled. What were they going to do, plant a garden? But before I could say anything, men's angry and taunting shouts filled the air. They were demanding Lot's presence in the street.

Lot looked at us with a deathly pallor and said in a trembling voice, "My Lord, with your permission, I will go and see what it is that they want." With this, he turned and quickly walked towards the street gate at the end of the yard, his path lit with lamps placed intermittently along the wall. I looked at Gabriel and shrugged, Lot didn't look like he could handle anything. The mob was going to lynch him and come for us, and then the party was going to start, but we had to protect him and keep him from getting himself killed until then.

I sighed and glanced sideways at Gabriel. "I was looking forward to tea and rice cookies."

The shouts from the crowd were getting louder and more threatening as they closed in on the house. I watched Lot stop at the gate, smooth out his robe, and then open it with authority. He immediately came face to face with a group of men – both young and old. The horde, which found it easy to be impertinent and unruly while the object of their malice was not present, instantly fell silent. Lot's posture and courage impressed me, and I felt the urge to go and stand by him. But I also wanted to find out what these men were capable of in order to get what they wanted. It would be the final justification that Gabriel and I needed. The silence was electric, but it did not last very long as a hulking brute of a man with curly, dark hair, beard and mustache, holding a massive club – what else could I expect – stepped forward and belligerently addressed Lot.

"Lot, where are the fine men who entered your house tonight? And don't say that you don't know, cause my little *weasel* here," he said, as he pulled the man from the court out from the group by the scruff of his robe, "followed you all the way home." He licked his lips provocatively and continued, "Now, send them out for us to have some fun, and maybe we'll let you play, too. It's been too many nights without new entertainment." The hulk leaned forward and said in a hoarse whisper, "I'm especially interested in the one who smashed my statue. He will like what I have waiting for him; the real thing." With that, he slammed the end of the club in to the palm of his shovel-like hand and stood staring down at Lot for a second. Then, slowly, he turned his head and looked directly at where Gabriel and I were standing, as if he knew. "Come out, come out, wherever you are. I have what you're looking for. And if you don't want it, well too bad."

"Banner, please don't do this. They are not ordinary men, but angels from heaven. They have come to save us!"

Lot's plea fell on deaf ears and did nothing to distract Banner from his immediate goal. He looked back at his companions and snickered. The effect was contagious as the mob started to laugh and jeer. Banner turned to look at Lot.

"Yeah, and I'm the devil incarnate! Now, send your *honorable* guests out or we'll have to go in and get them," he said, and added as an afterthought, "and anything else that we find interesting."

Despite the warm summer evening, Lot shivered, as if a chill had just gone through him. His eyes darted back and forth between the man standing in front of him and the mob waiting to attack. It was obvious that Banner was looking for trouble. No one ever dared deny him anything, and he loved a good confrontation. Breaking men and taking what he wanted was his favorite pastime. Lot, still standing at the gate, took a step forward and, as unobtrusively as possible, swung the gate shut behind him as he replied, "I beg of you, please reconsider. I will fetch my daughters. They are young, beautiful and completely unblemished. You can have them, surely they will be to your pleasure."

"Lot, Lot, it's as if you don't even know me."

Banner grunted and moved forward. He roughly pushed Lot aside, raised his foot and slammed it into the gate with the strength of a bull. The hinges holding the gate exploded as it swung open and smashed against the wall, shattering the lamp lighting the entrance, and then fell to the ground. Lot scrambled sideways, tripped, and hit the wall with ferocious intensity. The shock caused him to lose his balance and, half unconscious, he collapsed. It's at these moments that legends are born – later to become exaggerated fantasies and superstitions, but before he was even close to hitting the ground, in a flash of blue light, I was there beside him. I caught Lot under the arms and gently sat him down with his back to the gate wall. At that same instant, Gabriel appeared at the entrance where the gate had been standing just moments before. He looked bewildered but, now, absolutely committed to our mission and what needed to be done. I knelt beside Lot and gritted my teeth as he slowly rubbed his forehead and came to, his eyes focusing on my face. Unlike Gabriel, although I was itching to strike and destroy unceremoniously, my drive was not fueled by empathy for or any connection to Lot. It was simply fed by Man's venal nature; a being with a soul so noble and divine, yet with a mind so feeble and corruptible that any seed planted by a hellion like Lucifer would readily grow and flourish.

"Lot, go inside. We'll take it from here," I ordered.

From behind me, Banner roared with amusement, "Are *these* the angels you were talking about? They don't look very heavenly. Where are their wings and silky, curly hair?" He moistened his lips and continued, "But I have to admit, that one over there," motioning to Gabriel, "is definitely to our taste. And this one," he said, while standing over me, "must be the badass who defaced my statue. Well, he won't be a badass much longer." The men in the crowd behind him shouted and cheered their approval and started to push forward.

I looked up at Gabriel and hissed venomously, "And *these* are the men Abraham was pleading for? I think not, for their souls are beyond salvation." I stood and turned to face Banner and the crowd, my black overcoat swishing behind me. At that moment, the whole of my attention was centered on the man standing so defiantly in front of me. Anyone with that much mass would not be afraid of anything, but as I recalled the mouse and the elephant, I grinned and said in a malefic tone, "The moment of redemption has arrived. Mother Earth shall receive that which is rightfully hers; lots and lots of ashes."

With my eyes fixed on my prey, I extended my arm and pointed to a building across the street. There wasn't anything particularly outstanding about the two story structure except for its size and the glowing, red lamps lighting the doorway and multitude of dimly lit, draped windows. The building started to emanate a bluish glow against the darkness surrounding it. At that moment, almost as if on cue, the smell of the burning oil that had spilled when the gate shattered the lamp hit me, and served as a reminder of what the night held in store. I grimaced as the blue light momentarily intensified just before the building exploded into a fiery mass. The crowd, stunned by the explosion, immediately stopped and fell silent. They watched in disbelief as fire consumed the building within seconds and roared against the night sky. There were no survivors. Banner's attention, however, did not waver from me. He lifted the club above his head and lunged.

"You're mine, you miserable freak!"

The club crashed down on my right shoulder with such brutality and force that it exploded from within, its wooden fibers torn asunder. An ordinary man would have been instantly maimed, if not killed, by that blow. But I'm not that puny – as another hulk of a man would in the future say to a similar godly adversary. To me, the attack was no more than an annoying fly on a raging bull, and I wanted him to know that. It felt good to be the bull against the bully. I calmly brushed the broken wood pieces from my shoulder and grinned.

"You have to do better than that, Banner," I said in a sardonic tone. "Maybe you should try something other than a toothpick?"

Banner stared at me in disbelief. It was obvious that he wasn't used to being challenged – at least not physically, and this wasn't a game of chess. In a frenzy, he threw down what remained of the club, screamed with rage and punched me in the chest. To his surprise, there was no impact. His fist went right through and disappeared inside me, a halo of blue light surrounding his arm where the point of contact would have been. Immediately, the world around us faded and went silent as a mass of whirling wind enveloped us and created an impenetrable vortex. It was our own personal prison.

"Welcome to your party, Banner!"

Horrified, Banner whipped his head from side to side and unsuccessfully tried to pull his arm free. He tugged and wrenched repeatedly, and with each try his face aged years, the exertion consuming his life energy. He screamed in terror as he watched his once mammoth-like body shrivel like an old prune, and his towering stature bend forward like an old twig. His hair and beard became grizzly and thin while his eyes sunk into their sockets, and his skin lost all the radiance of youth and health. He was now an old man, with an old man's face, all wrinkled and leather-like, but grotesque and without any lines of timely wisdom. He was in touch with death, and well, that just sucks for anything living.

I grabbed his face and forced him to look at me. His would be the first soul to be taken that night. But then, to my surprise, the contorted and deathly metamorphosis stopped. Banner's body relaxed and his eyes grew thin and ice cold. His stare, now, was a piercing challenge. Suddenly, I felt his hand move inside my chest, his fingers digging their way to my heart, grasping it and slowly closing into a vice-like grip. I was too shocked to react, much less try to understand how this was possible. My breathing became more and more labored as Banner tightened his hold. My face seared in pain as if cut in half with a dull, serrated knife, and I could feel the blood crawl to a stop in my veins. I looked down. My hands and fingers were completely white and withered. They were dying from inside and would soon start to decay.

"You really thought that on a momentous night such as this I would not be here? How *naïve*. It's *our* party, now, brother."

The tone behind that voice was unmistakable, and although I still expected to see Banner when I looked up, the eyes boring into mine were much more lethal and threatening.

"Lucifer!"

I violently grabbed what used to be Banner's wrist and with a powerful twist broke it. His fingers relaxed and I yanked his hand from my chest. The relief was immediate, and I was able to breathe normally again as blood rushed through my veins, and my hands regained their color. I looked at Banner's distorted figure standing in front of me, but all I could see was Lucifer's arrogant smile – Faust got a good deal when he sold his soul, Banner not so much. Possessed souls are utterly destroyed, and although Man cannot see the change, the destruction is always visible to me. My eyes instantly burned with raw energy, and radiated with searing, blue heat.

"How dare you interfere?" I spat. "But I don't know why I'm surprised, because nothing that you do has any hint of morality or dignity anymore. Not even to wait for the condemned."

"Bla, bla, bla… stop whining, little brother. You know I'm as impatient as a goat. And, more importantly, I couldn't let you steal what is rightfully mine, now could I?" Lucifer looked smug. He knew that his presence alone annoyed me, but that was never enough. He never lost an opportunity to push my buttons. "If I'm not mistaken, and I never am, your Lord and Master – whom you have to blindly obey, mind you – ordered you to burn the cities of Sodom and Gomorrah to the ground such that *no one* remained! I believe that by no one He included Lot and his family, don't you?"

Ordinarily, if anyone else made that remark, I would stop to consider. But because it was Lucifer, there was no way in hell. Anything from him, even the wisest comment or compliment did nothing but irritate me, and his mere presence was enough to get my blood pressure so high that any mortal would have a massive coronary. In this case, I heard the blood rushing through my ears and felt it forcefully expand its pathway as it pumped through my veins. I bared my teeth and with my right hand engulfed in blue flames, backhanded him across the face with all I had. Lucifer plunged sideways off balance and crashed into the spiraling vortex prison that surrounded us. The resulting explosion was deafening as the vortex dissolved, releasing the concentrated power that had been contained in a whirlpool of twisting and churning energy. Both of us were violently thrown backwards through the air as the shockwave spread out in waves. I landed on the stone street with a bone crunching thud, but immediately got to my feet, looking around as I did so. Lucifer was nowhere to be seen. The crowd, however, was thrown in every direction and men lay sprawled on the ground, some on top of each other, unconscious or groaning in pain. I watched in silence, my senses sharp and attuned to the situation. The fight with Lucifer was far from over, and he always fought dirty.

I stood with my arms slightly spread out and ready to attack. There was nothing; he was nowhere. Then, I felt the earth tremble ever so slightly and knew that Lucifer was about to make his move. He was coming for me from hell. But before I could pinpoint the origin of the tremor, Lucifer emerged from the ground behind me, and he was definitely on fire. Even with my back to him, it was impossible not to notice the blinding light of his aura or the intensity of the heat that emanated from his being. In my mind's eye, I saw his body glowing, consumed by flames and shooting fire up into the starry night. I stood still and cursed myself for letting him have the upper hand once again. There was no way for me to turn and attack fast enough, so I bowed my head in an attempt to protect it from the oncoming onslaught, and focused my energies on shielding my back. I knew he was going to be merciless, just as I would be. I closed my eyes and prayed that my shield would protect me long enough against his fire to give me a chance to launch my own assault. Once again, I was mistaken.

"That fancy hand glowing crap might scare these lowlife mortals, but unless you're the Holy Father himself, get ready for another lesson."

Lucifer sprang with blinding speed, a panther going for the jugular. He grabbed me by the collar, his hand a burning globe of fire, and with a mighty tug lifted me off my feet. That definitely wasn't what I expected, so my shield did nothing to protect me, and before I could react, he swung me around in an arc and sent me flying like a rag doll. I tried to regain my balance, but he lifted his free hand and I knew that I was outsmarted. I was flying through the air backwards, actually facing him, and saw his eyes glow red as a fireball exploded from his outstretched palm and spearheaded its way towards me. In a desperate attempt to minimize the damage, I twisted my body around for more protection, but my efforts were useless as the fireball rapidly grew in size and filled my vision. The impact was inevitable, and I bellowed in frustration as I was engulfed by its heat. Infuriated by my miscalculation and terrified at my vulnerability, the only thing that I could do in that split-second was to cross my arms in front of me to form a sort of shield. The impact of the fireball against my arms and chest was bone crushing, the heat so intense that it actually felt ice cold. I thought I was being cut to pieces. I was in agony, but the assault on my body wasn't over. At that instant, I crashed backwards into the side of a house, the stone and wood shattering, splinters cutting and piercing every part of my body as I flew through leaving a gaping hole in my wake. My landing wasn't any better, and I hit the ground with a loud crunch and bounced off just to slam into the opposite wall and finally come to rest. I barely had time to move a muscle before the house was bombarded by countless fireballs. Doors were torn off their hinges and windows exploded, sending fragments of wood, stone and glass in every direction. The walls shuddered and then suddenly collapsed, burying me in the fiery wreckage.

THIRTEEN

The extermination of Sodom and Gomorrah had started. And although not what we originally planned, Michael took the destruction of the house as the signal to begin the assault. The night sky, moments before black and filled with stars, was now a blazing orange as thousands of brimstone meteors streaked down and relentlessly pelted the city. Houses and buildings were torn apart with merciless brutality. The Lord's wrath, its level of aggression, was breathtaking in its savagery. The whole city was on fire, flames whipping up tens of meters into the air from burning buildings and destroyed streets. Everything was pure chaos. People, young and old, ran in all directions, from houses into the streets and from the streets into houses, hoping to find some kind of refuge from the raining fire. But there was no escape. Soon, every house and building was pummeled to the ground and the streets were mazes of fire. Countless bodies lay charred and buried in the rubble or were strewn across the glowing streets, the sky above an angry red, and above that, the heavens lost in smoke. No one was immune; no one escaped.

Gabriel, with Lot and his family behind him, raced to the courtyard that led to the city gates. The fire in the streets had spread quickly, fanned by the wind coming from the north, and the path was barely passable. Most of the houses were already in flames and the thick, black smoke made visibility and breathing very difficult. Suddenly, the front door of one of the remaining houses leading to the gate was yanked open, and a man stumbled out and fell to his knees. He looked back at the house and in between coughs, desperately called for someone. Gabriel instinctively rushed forward to help, but Lot's alarmed cry made him stop. Before he could do anything else, the row of houses exploded into nothingness. But in that last instant before the explosion, the man looked at him and Gabriel saw the despair and fear that death brings. And it's in those last precious moments that the soul can plead for salvation; but not this time. In a flash, it was all over.

Gabriel turned to Lot, "You have to leave, *now*! Take your family and go. And do not look back for anything. Let this be the proof of your detachment from this city of sin so that you may be spared."

"But the people? Who will save the people?" Lot asked. His eyes were red and tears ran down his face uncontrollably.

"There is no hope for them. I'm sorry," said Gabriel. "Now *go*! Leave before it's too late. There is only so much that we can do to keep you safe." He grabbed Lot by the arm and pushed him down the street leading to the gates. Lot's wife and daughters scrambled behind him. It was the end of the line for Gabriel, because now it was all on them. Redemption is fickle and has no tolerance for selfishness and if there was to be any salvation for any of them, it would depend on their actions in the next few minutes. Lot turned and momentarily stared in the direction of where home had been, and then grabbed his family and without hesitation ran. Within seconds, they were gone, lost in the smoke.

FOURTEEN

The sky above Sodom and Gomorrah was filled with millions of live sparks of burning wood that rained down like shooting stars. Hell itself could be no hotter. But none of this mattered; life in all its forms and manifestations had ceased to exist and was extinguished from every corner of the cities. Earthly life, that is, for Lucifer stood in the middle of the destruction where Lot's house used to be with flames lapping at him from every direction. He looked irate, the knowledge of being tricked gnawing at his gut, but he was not fazed. The offense simply made him more determined to collect his prize; *every* single soul. I could see his back from where I was buried under the smoldering rubble. Slowly, I pushed the burnt wood and other debris aside and, through the smoke and haze, got to my feet. My face was dirty and stung where blood dripped from dozens of cuts. I was completely covered with soot, my overcoat burning at the edges and my hair singed into a tangle, its offending sulfurous smell filling my nose. I opened my arms and embraced the fire in utter defiance of the very element that defined Lucifer and let out a low, feral growl as my wings unfolded behind me. My eyes narrowed into slits of animalistic fury.

"Lucifer!"

The vicious mention of his name, threatening enough to chill the bones of any being, didn't evoke any reaction from Lucifer. But it should have, because he and I both knew that it was hurt time. Instead, he just stood there with his back to me, lifted his arms and massaged his chest. Then, in a very casual tone, he said, "I can always count on your stubbornness. But you still don't understand that although you're tough, I'm tougher. And smarter."

I didn't wait to see what would happen next. It was what he expected from me and that predictability made him, in turn, be predictable and I knew exactly what to do. I dashed forward and closed the distance between us with lightning speed. Lucifer did not move a muscle and maintained his confident and annoying calm. His smug attitude confirmed my suspicions, nevertheless it also fueled my anger – a definite mistake since anger is his prayer – and I grabbed him from behind with such violence that his bones and muscles cracked and tore. Lucifer's demeanor, however, stayed the same. I looked over his shoulder and saw that I was right. There, held in his grip was a smoldering fireball, his weapon of choice. I grinned as my wings enveloped him, closing him in a feathered, but ironclad prison, and lifted him up and off his feet. Then, with a mighty shove, I thrust my body straight up and shot skywards with my captive. Lucifer didn't resist, he smiled and enjoyed the ride.

"How long did it take before you recovered from our last fight? If I'm not mistaken, and I *never* am, it was a good century before you could fly with dignity again."

I gritted my teeth. The memory of our previous battle was not something that I liked to be reminded of, especially since Lucifer blindsided me because I was too naïve to believe that he would attack me from behind – or at all, for that matter. But the pain and humiliation served to harden me, and I got wise to his relentless character. Lucifer never gives up, and since our war was not yet so defined, he made it a point to win every battle or, at the least, deliver the last blow. His beating me senseless – almost two hundred years after Abel's murder – was a lesson and payback for Cain; and it was the only lesson I ever needed.

"This time, I'll make sure you stay grounded with your mortal friends even longer."

There was a thunderous but muddled explosion as Lucifer detonated the fireball. The fierceness of the blast made my wings shake violently and expand to the point where the pain became almost unbearable. I bellowed in anger and frustration as my shoulders and wing joints started to rip, and for a split second I thought that it would be a repeat of last time. But suddenly, the intensity of the attack was over and my wings held.

"Seems like I've learned a few new tricks. And, yes, I do remember last time, just as you will remember this one! Sometimes it pays to be stubborn."

I can't explain how enjoyable it was to watch Lucifer savagely try to break free from his winged cocoon. His soul – not really sure if he still had one – was on fire. With his arms bent and pinned against his chest, he had no other option but to forcefully throw his shoulders from left to right and thrash against the walls of his prison as he tried to break or weaken my grip. But I had prepared for this, and there was nothing that he could do in that position to overpower me. His arrogance had cost him this round. He played his card and lost. The roar that emanated from his mouth was bestial, and his face contorted into a mass of fury as he transformed from his human form. He glared back at me with the blood, red eyes of the diabolical beast he'd become – red skin, bulging muscles, horns, fangs, tail and all – and growled contemptuously, baring his yellow teeth ready to attack, rip and tear. I sneered back and waited for his next move as we continued to climb. Lucifer hissed, his forked tongue flicking in and out, and then slumped in resignation. Defeated? Only when hell freezes over. But for now it was as good as it gets.

"Temperamental, aren't we? And we haven't even talked business; about the souls that I snatched right from under your nose."

I wanted to continue feeding his rage and push him to the edge. But this was his territory, and Lucifer's mind was too contorted, and his being way too slippery to play into my very obvious strategy. He shrugged and made himself comfortable, accepting his temporary role as prisoner. We both knew this wasn't going to last long, so he didn't have to react and assumed his usual cold, calculating self and didn't give me the satisfaction of engaging. Instead, he exhaled slowly and said matter-of-factly, "You know that you can't do that. They were all condemned by your Lord, so how can you explain disobeying Him? Your orders were to simply chastise and abandon everyone to me." But I knew he didn't accept defeat lightly – or at all, for that matter – even if it was momentary, and behind the cool of it all, I felt his body tremble almost imperceptibly with suppressed anger.

Now, what he said, he believed, but I was enjoying the victory and felt no need to respond. I guess I had learned more from Lucifer than I imagined. Keeping quiet can sometimes be the most explosive weapon. I felt his muscles tighten and knew that he was seething inside.

"They belong to me!"

Hearing the frustration behind those four words made me smile. I genuinely felt elated for the first time in centuries. It was definitely redemption time, and as I accelerated towards heaven, I felt myself completely recharged and knew that this proximity would cause Lucifer great distress and even ebb away at his powers. But life, even an archangel's life, is a journey of mostly sour grapes, and the hero seldom wins. Not that I think that I'm a hero, but I'd like to believe that I'm better than Lucifer.

Anyway, my elation was cut short as my attention was drawn to a point beyond the city gates. Lucifer noticed and followed my gaze. What I saw was not disturbing or frightening, just disappointing to me and delightful for him. Life, when remembered as a story, is a tale told by an idiot, and the romanticized account of it is a tale told by an even greater idiot – at least a friend of mine in the future would immortalize this thought in writing. But Man likes to tell tales, so we call them romantics, and I was once a romantic believing in happy endings.

I focused my attention on Lot and his family as they ran from the burning city – and although I knew it in my mind – realized for the first time in my heart that I was looking at the sole survivors of two cities. Cities that had taken centuries to build but mere instants to obliterate. Sodom and Gomorrah had ceased to exist and would soon be buried under the desert sand never to be found.

Lot and his two daughters were huddled together and walked quickly and with determination in the direction of the hills. I was surprised, since I imagined them to be the ones who would fail. However, it was Lot's wife who had separated and was walking melancholically in their wake, her gait full of uncertainty and doubt. Could I save her? Snatch her from Lucifer's grip as I did with Cain? But as I looked down, I knew that it was already too late. Lucifer, even in his imprisoned condition, stirred the seed of passion and desire in her, whispering in her ear what her heart yearned for, burned for. *"Don't listen! You can fight him!"* I shouted in my mind as she stopped, slowly turned her head, reached out her arm towards the burning city and then instantly turned into a pillar of salt. How ironic, the same salt that she had borrowed earlier from her neighbors to prepare food for us.

Lucifer laughed hysterically, and although it was not a complete victory, with Lot and his daughters safe and beyond his grasp, that moment was sweeter than any that he had ever experienced over me. For him, destroying that momentary elation that I felt was priceless. He always wanted to prove that my choice to serve Father rather than join forces with him was the wrong choice, and that Man was essentially greedy and selfish. There was no salvation.

"My, my. Another one bites the dust. Who would have guessed? I did!"

It's impressive how Lucifer could turn the tables on me by saying exactly the kind of thing that got under my skin, but I don't think he expected what was coming. Suddenly, everything was different. This beast that I had once called brother got to me, yet again, and ripped that small twinkle of happiness from me and tore it to pieces. I lost control and let compulsion and hatred replace reason. I had no cunning plan – and I was not the Black Vegetable. There was no strategy, no tactic, and no instance of morality or talk; just hatred. I released Lucifer and pushed him down. He must have thought that I wanted to get away from him because he looked up at me and sneered. But I was on top of him like lightning, pummeling him, my fists and knees mercilessly ramming his body and face. Lucifer, dazed and disoriented, fell through the sky like dead weight. But I wasn't done. I dived after him, gripped his wrist and violently pulled him up, hammering his chest with my free hand at the same time. He exhaled, the breath knocked out of him. But again, this was Lucifer and he wasn't going to give up that easily. Slashing out, he grabbed my neck, his yellowish claws digging in, tearing the skin, causing damage. I screamed in pain and jerked sideways as I gripped the assaulting hand in an iron-like brace and twisted it. There was a loud crunch as his wrist broke. The beast howled, pulling back and recovering his hand. With the ground only meters away, I lifted both legs and savagely sledgehammered them into his chest, sending him crashing into the dirt with such force that even Mother Earth groaned. The impact was inhuman, and the ground under Lucifer cracked in every direction like slithering snakes, the fiery remnants of what used to be houses exploding into the air as the shockwaves hit them. Lucifer's body lay battered and bleeding, buried in a crater in the center of the destruction to the destruction. I landed with an authoritative thud beside him and looked down. As I stood there looming over him, I felt no remorse. To the contrary, my senses were acute and I felt a cool calm. Lucifer, bloody and in pain, laboriously gasped for air as he rose to his feet. But I still wasn't finished with him. I kicked his legs out from under him, making him fall. He landed on his back, groaned wearily, his body bruised and broken, and stared at the starry sky above him. He was breathing in spurts, and a bloody foam oozed from his lips.

"Time to make this memorable, you old goat."

I looked down at Lucifer and our eyes locked momentarily, the red of fire and passion versus the blue of what used to be faith and integrity. There would be no truce, not now, not ever. I nodded as my eyes focused on Lucifer's horns, and I felt an uncharacteristic moment of tranquil coldness and immediately knew what I was going to do. It was the desecration of a symbol, the breaking of an unspoken bond, an unthinkable act, and yet, the ultimate reward. I smiled, somewhat in the vein of how Lucifer smiled when he had you in his crosshairs, lifted my booted foot and brought it down hard on Lucifer's left horn. The horn shattered into pieces, the explosion of energy thunderous and lethal, but not colossal enough to dwarf the blood curdling howl that emanated from Lucifer's mouth. I stood there and watched him writhe in pain, but the moment did not last as he regained his usual arrogant composure and stared up at me.

"You shouldn't have done that, brother." Lucifer was emphatic, but his tone was low and cold, too matter-of-factly cold. It caused me to tense up, but I simply shrugged and turned to leave. I knew that by breaking his horn I had escalated our battles to a full blown war. "This time you went too far. I vow to you that, even if it takes an eternity, I will have your soul for this." Lucifer stared as I walked away, then murmured with a grin, "And you will give it to me of your own accord."

A. A. Bavar

FIFTEEN

The days – for Man, it was more than a millennia to be exact – that followed Sodom and Gomorrah were quite uncharacteristic. Manipulation and always having the upper hand was what defined Lucifer, so I expected revenge to be his top priority. I anticipated him to jump out of every dark corner and unceremoniously deliver my punishment. In truth, I wanted him to react as I would and lash out in fury without a plan or scheme, and simply get it over with. But that's not his way, and soon it became clear that he was going to wait things out, and like a snake in the grass, seek the opportune moment to strike. His threat to have my soul gnawed at me temporarily, but it was so ludicrous, so impossible, that I shrugged it off – a fatal mistake, since disregarding Lucifer is like a sheep walking in to a wolf's den believing that they can coexist. The seed was planted, and it was just a matter of time, but I was arrogant and sure that I would never do the one thing that would deliver me to him. But never is a long time, and as my friend Dickens said, "Never say never."

All of this, however, suddenly became unimportant as Man, once again, managed to astound and bewilder me. How could he venerate and worship all sorts of idle Gods and imagery and then fail to see His true manifestation? It was a dark day when I descended on Golgotha ready to obliterate and destroy without mercy. The rocky hill where the crucifixion had taken place was barren and deserted, its caves resembling hollow eye sockets that made it look like a half buried skull looking down at that grotesque scene. A tenebrous image cast its shadow towards the east wall of the city of Jerusalem as people scurried past the Place of the Skull – the hill of death – to the city gate. This was a place for the violent and the dishonest, the assassin and the murderer, where they were dragged and punished beyond measure until I came and relieved them. And the scene was no different today, although it could not be any more wrong.

Three men on crucifixes, their hands and feet nailed to the wood, suffered the scalding heat of the early afternoon sun. I saw Bran drift below me and circle the space above one of them, and I knew it must be the lowlife, Gestas. How dare they put my Lord brother beside a wretch like *him*? His taunts against Jesus, even as he hung there dying, rang in my ears. Did he really think that by goading my brother He would save him? But he paid for his insults with eternal silence and pain. Bran would take his tongue, and Lucifer would burn his soul forever while he screamed only for his mind to hear. At that moment, however, not even Bran had the heart to face my brother; but he would do his job soon enough.

Jesus was the most tortured, His body mutilated by flagellation with a deep gash on His chest that bled profusely. A crown of thorns was placed around His head as humiliation, cutting deep into His flesh as blood ran down His face and through His eyes. He, however, was tranquil and serene showing no signs of anguish or grief. To the contrary, He was calm and dignified, with a demeanor that was anything but earthly.

With what energy He had left, Jesus looked up to the clear skies and said, "My God, my God, why have you forsaken me?"

My eyes burned with tears as I heard those words, and I fell through the sky in His direction. As I approached, the sadness that consumed me cast such a blanket of gloom across the bright sky that you could feel the void of life and happiness. Its inky darkness crawled like a plague from the foot of Golgotha to the city of Jerusalem, and the heavens rumbled with grief as erratic explosions lit the sky, and the angels' tears rained down amidst the crack of each lightning.

I landed with great force at the foot of the cross that held my brother, but couldn't bring myself to look up. Bran landed on my shoulder and cawed. The ground was wet and rivulets of blood ran down the hill. I remained with my head bowed and my long hair and wings dripping as they loosely hung to the ground. The smell of burned soil and electrified air filled the blackness as the storm intensified and punished the ground around us with hail and lightning. I felt like a savage beast trapped in a cage, consumed with both fear and rage; wanting vengeance but knowing that there also had to be justice. At that instant, there was a flash of lightning followed by an earsplitting scream.

"It is the Archangel of Darkness come to take us!" wailed Dismas, using the last of his energies before he passed out.

I exhaled in disgust and slowly turned my head up and towards the offending creature, but a slight movement by Jesus caught my attention and I froze. Our eyes locked. The sight of my brother, so brutally abused and dishonored, made me gasp. Only once before, with Abel's murder, had I felt this lost, but this time I couldn't blame Lucifer. This time it was all on Man. I jumped from the ground and perched on top of Gestas's cross. Bran hopped from my shoulder to my knee and onto the beam directly above his head. Gestas twisted his head up and repeatedly shrieked in terror, as if my being there made any difference to his end; or maybe he was just deathly afraid of crows. Either way, he was not penitent; just terrorized. His heart was infested and there was no redemption, and the screaming was very annoying. I pointed my finger at him and made the sign of a cross – another one for Man and the ages – and immediately time stopped. There was no movement or sound; everything earthly was in a void.

"This one," I said, and patted Gestas on the head, "will be a pleasure to give as a gift to Lucifer. The other? Well, lucky him to believe in you just when it matters." I stopped and once again looked at Jesus, and although I was trying to be the archangel that my brother envisioned, the indignation and contempt that I felt was overwhelming. Still in my perched position, I stretched my arms in a wide and world embracing gesture and cried in a guttural whisper, "As for this! This heinous and deplorable act, the punishment *will* fit the crime. I'll put the fear of *me* in every soul. Humanity will feel, then hear, and then see me come. Sodom and Gomorrah will be child's play by the time I'm done with Man this time."

Jesus looked from me to Jerusalem and his eyes shimmered with tears. He knew me well and understood that my rage would not be curbed by mere persuasion; even by him. "Is this what Father wishes? To destroy humanity for my sake?"

"He was too saddened to *wish* for anything, so I took charge. Somehow, I don't think He would object to what I have in mind." There was no doubt, I was fully committed to punishing humanity despite its implications. Lucifer had won this battle; he could have all the souls he wanted; again. "I love you, brother, but I don't love mankind. And mankind is so unlike you."

Jesus cautiously moved his head to the side, looked to the heavens and said, "Father, forgive them, for they know not what they do," and then he turned to me and continued, "Into your hands I commit my passage."

I was totally bewildered. There was nothing more that I wanted at that moment but to unleash my fury on humanity and seek justice for my brother. But then, the wisdom of Jesus's action became clear to me. He had in a single, selfless and uncompromising act absolved humanity of its sins and thwarted Lucifer. I had a lot to learn. For the first time in many days, I allowed myself a meek smile, there would be more than enough time in the future for retribution.

SIXTEEN

"When I walked into the Room of Candles today, I knew that it was a significant day. I can always tell when something momentous is about to happen, but I never imagined that today marked the end of *me*." I looked down at the leaf with the letter *M* inscribed on it. "*M*," I said, "also stands for the name Mary." There was an involuntary gasp, and for the first time, I heard the robed figure react. But that was it, and silence immediately shrouded her once more.

I decided that today's events could wait, I had to start from the beginning; with Mary. I looked at her and our eyes met, and in the dim light I felt her gaze. "My encounter with Mary was very unique – there's no other way to describe it, and our paths became intertwined in the most unusual way." I paused and looked down at my hands. They were shaking, and the fury that I had felt that morning surged again. Once more, I wanted to tear into and destroy everything in my path. I gritted my teeth and continued, "I had become a soul gathering machine with no compassion or love left in me for humanity. The lesson of selflessness and love that I had learned from Jesus had long been washed away by the plagues of war and destruction instigated by Man. What kept me going was the satisfaction I felt in opposing Lucifer – and of course, it didn't hurt

when I could visit a Vlad or a Hitler and unleash the fear of God in them."
I stopped and shook my head. Even to me that sounded insensitive and narcissistic, but it was who I had become.

"I had lost my connection with the meaning of life – and the spiritual significance of life after death, what did that matter? Everything had become so overshadowed by death and the atrocities that caused death – and of course, with Lucifer as the permanent puppet master, all that I looked for *was* death." I stopped and took a deep breath. "That's when I met Mary for the first time. My soul was dead to humanity, but she gave me a present that showed me what I had closed my eyes to, and for nineteen years I was happy, truly happy. Until today."

I looked down at the darkened surface of the oak table and was suddenly somewhere else, looking down at another table covered with thousands and thousands of inscribed leaves. The room I was looking at was in absolute silence and lighted only by a single lamp placed on the table. The lamps on the walls were off, and by the look of it – the amount of dust and cobwebs, the room had been neglected for many years. I was sitting with my head bowed, elbows resting on the table and lost amidst the leaves, with my hands clasped together under my chin. Suddenly, there was a swish of air and a loud thud. Leaves and dust flew everywhere and it made the already half lit room even more gloomy.

"I've been looking for you." Michael loomed just inches from me. I didn't move or look up, but instead stared down at his boots. They were cool, the way the black leather was etched with spiraling curves and lines. I wondered when he had ditched his sandals and finally entered the twenty-first century. But I guess if Moses could part the seas then Michael could also change.

"Well, you found me. And it wasn't as if I was hiding." Without looking at him, I waved my arm and motioned around the room, and then continued, "This is where I spend most of my time. How hard were you looking? Anyway, what is it that you want?"

"Isn't it obvious? Look at all these souls waiting for a chance at redemption. You cannot ignore your duty."

"I haven't ignored anything. They have other means. They can always pray to Father, and if they haven't, well maybe they don't deserve salvation. I'm on a break from humanity."

"You're on a break? What the hell does that mean? That Lucifer wins? This is ludicrous, especially because it was he who warned you about being too rash with the oath that you took by Abel." Michael was practically yelling, although I could tell that he was trying hard to control his temper. "Now, get up and take care of these souls before Lucifer does."

I've never responded well to orders, and it wasn't going to be this time that I would. Michael slammed his clenched fist on the table. "I said, get *up!*"

I slowly looked up at him and paused for a short moment before I replied. "As I said, I'm on a break. But it's quite clear that you won't let this go, even though you don't understand or have the faintest idea what this is," I said, and grabbed a handful of leaves and threw them up in front of him. "So, before you judge me and tell me of the oath I took on that god-forsaken day, make sure you can handle the burden."

"I'm not judging anyone, just reminding you of your responsibilities. And if it's a burden, then it's your cross to bear and no one else's."

I nodded and stood up. Michael's face was mere inches from mine. We stood there for a few seconds, but there really wasn't anything else to say. He was mad, but what did I care? For me to get mad or feel anything at all, I would have to care, and I didn't. I felt nothing, everything was a vacuum. Well, maybe that's not entirely true, because I did want him to feel my pain – my *cross*, as he had put it. I pushed him aside and walked to the center of the room.

"Offer these souls a chance to repent, you say?" I said, as I turned to face him once again. "I can do that, but I'm quite positive that you will not get the result you're hoping for." I took a deep breath and simultaneously moved my arms in an upward motion. The leaves that were scattered on the floor and strewn about the room started to tremble and then slide towards me. I stood there with my face turned to the ceiling and my arms held apart as intense blue sparks jumped form one hand to the other. It was all theatrics, since there was no celestial power to summon; *I* was the celestial force! But it looked cool and the outcome deserved it. The leaves started to swoosh in a circular path around me, and soon thousands of them were flying in the air like a tornado. I became engulfed and lost sight of Michael.

"This is Man created in Father's image; noble and virtuous," I shouted, as blue rays of electricity connected themselves to the whirling tornado and the whole thing became a cloudy blue mass. Immediately, it shaped itself into a human form and kneeled in front of me in reverent supplication.

"And now, mass redemption!" I pointed at the human figure and blasted it. The result was soul wrenching. A deafening mixture of screams, cries and shrieks filled the room – the pain, suffering and despair beyond measure. Michael covered his ears as tears rolled uncontrollably down his cheeks. The human figure fell to the floor and writhed from side to side as it broke apart and its pieces were consumed by fire – red fire. Suddenly, there was an explosion and then complete silence once again. The figure was gone, and with it all the souls. Michael was on his hands and knees, his body shaking as he tried to regain his composure. As I looked down at him, I felt a sting of guilt, but the knowledge that someone other than me had finally felt a fraction of the constant toil that I bore made it worthwhile. It reminded me a little of Dali, whose consciousness melted when he had a mere glimpse of his soul. But this was the Archangel Michael; he would recover in no time.

"What happened?" he asked in a low tone as he got to his feet.

"Nothing happened. Those souls were what they were and I simply put them on a bullet train to Gehenna. Now you know what it feels like to have the weight of humanity on your soul. I've been carrying it for thousands of years and I'm done." I was about to leave when to my surprise I saw a lonely leaf drop on the table. It had a bluish aura and was as unblemished as before. Michael noticed my surprise and followed my gaze. I walked to the table and picked it up. Inscribed on it in gold was the name Mary. I wasn't done after all, not just yet.

SEVENTEEN

Sometimes, I forget that when exceptional things happen, I should look over my shoulder and acknowledge Lucifer. Mary definitely fell into that category. The statement I had made was pretty damn solid, a definitive checkmate, and it would have freed me from my oath. I knew that Michael would explain things to Father, and any redemption that humanity wanted from that moment on they could ask for directly from Him. But now there was unfinished business, a deserving soul; a pure soul.

It was an evening in the spring of 1995, and the wind had picked up in New York City. I left immediately to fetch Mary, leaving Michael standing there by the table dazed and bewildered. I felt an excitement that was alien to me, and as I walked the street towards her house, I was consumed by a turmoil of thoughts. Mary wasn't a saint, prophet, or manifestation of God. She was Man created in the image of our Father. The same Man that was capable of tremendous love, compassion, and generosity, and yet, perpetuator of the greatest evil – to plunder, cheat and kill when left to his own devices. Contrary to popular belief, Lucifer is not sitting on Man's shoulder 24/7 tempting him; Man debases himself all on his own. And yet, Mary had survived the ultimate test and her soul had endured without being given the chance to repent or pray for salvation.

I was lost in these thoughts when I felt a presence in front of me and looked up just in time to stop myself from crashing into an old woman. I must have looked threatening, since she looked at me with wide open eyes that were twice their usual size and gasped. Old people, distant and close to birth at the same time.

"Not here for you this time either, Martha. When I am, you'll know, because it will be dark, cold and lonely. But I will make sure you go in the books as some kind of saint." Some people don't ever meet me, but this was the second time for Martha. I wondered if she recognized me and walked around her to the path that led to the front door of a stylish Victorian house. I stood there and stared at the knocker. I could just go to Mary, but decided to knock. I wanted to see how she lived and who she was before facing her. The sound of the knocker was loud and hollow, but was immediately followed by the patter of small feet running to the door. The door opened and I was scrutinized by a pair of big, brown eyes looking up at me. The little girl standing in the doorframe was no more than five, but lost no time to start her interrogation.

"Who are you? Did you come to get my mommy?"

"What? What did you say?"

"My mommy's sick again. She has to see the doctor, but I want to go, too. When I was sick, mommy gave me medicine that made my tummy all better. I want to tell the doctor to give mommy my medicine. But it tastes yucky, so we can't tell mommy. Okay?"

This was definitely not part of my plan. I should have gone straight to Mary. I looked down at the little girl and kneeled.

"What's your name?" I asked.

The little girl looked at me and frowned. I had violated some unknown rule and almost wished it was Lucifer that I had to contend with instead. I cleared my throat and decided to forget about the introductions.

"Mary is waiting for me. Can you take me to see her, little one?" *Little one?* I don't know what I was thinking, but panic would be the right definition if I knew what it was.

She pondered a moment and said, "I did a bad thing. Mommy says I should never open the door without asking." Then, as she turned and motioned for me to follow, she continued, "You have to take the hair off your face, mommy won't like that. And my name is Kay, for Kayleen!"

This was unique. I was being drilled and manhandled by a child. I walked in and followed Kay, barely paying attention to my surroundings. But all of a sudden, I felt a tremendous calm and as we walked through the brightly lit hallway, I noticed the faintest smell of jasmine and roses. Kay had a good home, a loving home.

We went up to the second floor and Kay stopped outside her mom's door and turned to look at me. I felt my heart skip a beat and hoped that she wouldn't start with the questions again.

"Mommy says, soon God will take care of her. Are you God? Will you take her to heaven?"

I stood there looking at her dumbfounded. What was it that this little creature wanted from me? I was ready to confess to anything if she would just stop asking questions. To my relief, we were interrupted.

"Kay, who are you talking to, honey?" asked Mary from inside the room.

Kay turned and marched in. I followed. Mary was in bed, propped up by pillows. There were two vases with roses in them, one on the bedside table and another by the window, and the room smelled like a rose garden.

"This man came to see you. I don't think he's a doctor. Doctors are all clean and wear white coats with lots of pens. I think he might be God, but he's all hairy and not glowy like the pictures."

It's not uncommon for children to sense the presence of angels or even connect with them in their dreams, but this was something unique. I felt her soul bond with me, and I knew that at some level Kay recognized who I was and she wasn't afraid.

Mary, however, did not acknowledge me and kept her eyes fixed on Kay. She was smiling.

"Kay, honey, please go and play in your room. Mommy needs to talk to the nice doctor alone."

"Okay, mommy. Can I have a cookie?"

"How about an apple? Let's keep *this* doctor away for as long as possible."

"Aww."

Kay took a step to leave but then stopped. She looked up at me and slowly walked to her mother's bed. Mary watched in silence as Kay carefully climbed up and lay down in her arms. It was only after Kay left the room that Mary looked at me for the first time since my arrival. With Kay gone, I felt my usual self – that perpetual anger took over – and although I was very curious about Mary, my feelings were once more guarded and locked. That brief moment of vulnerability and openness that Kay had aroused was gone, but not without leaving an impression. It had taken a while, but now I understood what a certain philosopher told me as he submissively awaited his fate in front of a firing squad for a punishment that far surpassed his crime; *the soul is healed by being with children.*

Mary wasn't shy or intimidated, and her eyes quickly found mine. I wanted to look away, but I couldn't. Those eyes were familiar to me, and her face reminded me of another face at another time. What had I walked into? What was this place? She beckoned me to approach and I obeyed. I stood by her bed and looked down.

"You're earlier than I had hoped. I thought maybe you would come later in the evening," she said, and smiled.

"You can see the truth. How interesting. It's been a very long time since someone saw me for who I am. And you're right, later would be more romantic. But there'll be no hero or dramatic final scene here. Just you and me," I said dryly, and immediately regretted my tone. I didn't want to be insensitive, not with her, but it was so natural. I cleared my throat and continued, "Did you have a happy life?"

Mary's eyes remained fixed on mine and did not waver for a second. There was trust, compassion, and love in her stare and I was the student.

"You still care, even if you feel like you don't want to."

Sometimes when the truth is staring us in the face, we fail to see it and lash out in frustration. For me, frustration was my status quo and I didn't know how else to respond but with anger.

"I think I have to reconsider my approach, because it's obvious that I'm not ominous looking enough to you. Damn the movies with all their special effects. Maybe if I was holding this," I said, as my scythe appeared in my grip. "*Now* do you fully realize who I am and why I'm here?"

"Yes, I do. Believe me. That's because we've met once before. You let me hold your finger."

I looked down at my hand, and there, wrapped around my index finger was a tiny hand. Millions and millions of souls and this was where our history had begun; a crashed car sinking in a river with baby Mary and her mother. The leaf I had that day was for Mary alone, and although the mother, in her delirious state, saw me and pleaded over and over for me to save her baby, that depended solely on the actions of other people. I was merely the courier, the angel you see when death is hanging on your shoulder. And it just happened that I was a bit early that day.

As I sat there in the back seat with Mary, who was strapped in her car seat and was unbelievably calm and amused by the water gushing in through the cracked driver's side window, the front of the car started to sink. Water slowly filled the interior and Mary's mother would soon be submerged. I looked on as she repeatedly tried to unlock her jammed seatbelt. Suddenly, she stopped her frantic efforts and looked at Mary, who was playing with my finger and trying to put it in her mouth. Then, she looked at me, and in that brief instant I felt her love and willingness to sacrifice her own life for that of her child. But there was nothing that I could do, it was beyond my control. I shook my head and witnessed how the tenderness that she felt for her child was replaced by unmeasurable grief and hatred towards me. But before she could say anything else, a man broke the passenger side window, cut the seatbelt and pulled her out of the sinking car. For a few moments, I heard her muffled cries, but that was soon replaced by eerie quietness.

Time was running out. In a few more seconds the car would sink.

"… take care of her for me…"

I heard the words and my eyes filled with tears, but they hadn't before, not on that day; not in a thousand years.

"… my daughter, Kay, watch over her…"

I looked up, and the sight of Mary all grown up shook me out of my reverie.

"Martha," I mumbled.

"No, Kay needs you. And your soul needs her even more."

EIGHTEEN

I never go to funerals, what's the point? It's like paying to go to the movies to watch the end credits. But this time I had to be there for Kay. Mary had cornered me twice, once with her chubby little fingers and a second time with a request she knew I would not refuse. It's not often that the angel of death connects with a mortal, and even less often that I don't take a soul after spending time with it. But nothing was kosher about that day, especially the suicidal rescue by a young boy. And although Man is known for having a soft spot for heroics, he's not necessarily a hero because he dies for it. In the end, another man's sacrifice saved Mary in those last few seconds and I ended up with a soul anyway.

So there I was, at Mary's funeral, feeling somber and nervous at the same time. The sadness that I felt about her death and Kay's loss was overshadowed by the petrifying feeling of being confronted by her questions. What did I know about kids, feelings and growing pains? As I walked the path to where the service was, I kept fiddling with the necklace and pendant in my overcoat pocket that Mary had given me to give to Kay. It was a message to Kay that she completely trusted me, and so should she. I was lost in these thoughts when I heard someone gulp in despair. I looked

to my side and saw the gardener staring at me and the path of dead flowers
and plants in my wake.

The group of people paying their last respects was small. Kay and
Martha were standing together by the headstone holding hands. I walked
up to them and softly called Kay. They both turned and I saw a sparkle of
joy mixed with a hint of uncertainty in Kay. Martha, on the other hand,
stumbled backwards, but managed to control her desire to run – that
always puts a smile on my face. She pulled Kay closer and tried to shield
her by pressing her body against hers. I looked at her and nodded, hoping
to reassure her that I wasn't there for her. She must have understood
because she relaxed her grip. I took out the necklace and kneeled down in
front of Kay.

"Hello, Kay."

Kay was staring at the necklace in my hand with a frown. "That's
Mommy's nine-pointed-star. How do you have it? Mommy said I could
have it. But I couldn't find it. Did you take it?"

"No, I didn't take it. Your mommy wanted me to keep it safe and
give it to you," I said, and held out my hand.

Kay didn't hesitate. She quickly stepped forward and put her hand
on top of the necklace in my hand. We remained like that for a few
seconds, hand in hand holding the necklace and then, without a word,
together we put the necklace around her neck.

"Mommy is with Daddy and God now. I don't think you're God anymore. See what I put on their headstone," she said, and pointed at the engraving.

The headstone was big, and it spanned both their graves. On it, in gold, was engraved, *Father And Mother, I Love You.* I looked at Kay and Martha and knew that I was part of her family, and soon would be her only family.

"Why are you sad? Are you going to say goodbye, like forever?"

"Yes and no," I said, and smiled. Confuse the child and open the door to a thousand more questions, why don't you, I thought to myself. But the truth was that I enjoyed it; enjoyed her. "I want to say goodbye to Mary, but never to you. Do you know what an angel is?"

Kay nodded.

"Well, I'm going to be your angel," I said with a smile, and held out my hand. "Hi, my name is Azrail and I'm very happy to be your friend."

Kay's eyes opened wide as she lifted her eyebrows, but then immediately scrunched them down into a frown. "Aziral? Azlirail? I *can't* say that!"

I put my hand back on my knee and gave a small chuckle. "Almost no one can, little one. There's never really any time for pleasantries when I'm around. But you can call me Az, how about that?" The question was redundant, I could see the answer shining in her eyes and it caused an overpowering feeling of something in me. I wanted to lift her in my arms and keep her there; protect her. But that was impossible, so I did the next best thing and made a promise which I ultimately failed to keep. "Whenever you need anything, if you're sad, if you're scared, or just want to see me, close your eyes and think of me and I'll be there before you know it," I said, then whispered almost solely to myself, "I'll protect you, little one."

Kay looked at me but did not react or say anything. Then, before I knew what was happening, she threw herself into my arms and I knew what that feeling was; love.

NINETEEN

That day in the cemetery sealed our relationship, and I became Kay's guardian, her new father figure. And although I never did anything that a human couldn't do, I made sure that she knew that I would always be there for her instantly. So, I became her go-to person for everything from getting tucked in for the night to helping with baby Barbie's diapers. But as much as I was a new, trusted friend for her, ultimately, she was the balm that healed *my* soul. Martha didn't approve at first, but she also had no choice. It was her child's dying wish, so she learned to accept it and eventually trust me.

The days, weeks, and months passed very quickly and soon it was time for the first day of school. I had been Man's guardian longer than time itself, but never had I felt worry or any anxiety on his behalf. On that day, however, I felt completely lost and for the first time had a glimmer of what being human involves. My thought processes, rational and calculating as always, were at war with my completely irrational feelings. And hard as I tried, the sense of loss and apprehension gnawed at me relentlessly because I knew that sometimes the heart senses what the mind fails to see. Martha suggested that I walk Kay to school, and that way relax a little and enjoy the moment. I agreed, and with her small backpack on her back – covered with sparkles, stars, and a pink unicorn, we set off. It was a short walk, and soon we were in the school yard. Kay was overjoyed at seeing the playground with so many swings and a huge monkey bar.

"Do you think I can play in the playground?"

I smiled, she was going to be fine. I was the one who needed therapy for separation anxiety. "I'm sure that your teacher has playing in the playground at the top of her list."

We walked into the school building and down the corridor to where Kay's classroom was located. Kay stopped just short of the door and for the first time that morning, held my hand. I felt my head sway, and for an instant Mary's chubby little fingers were once again wrapped around mine. It was that infinitesimal moment of reflection that reconciled my mind and heart and made me realize what was the driving force behind my uneasiness. It was not that it was too soon for Kay to leave the nest and explore the world on her own, but that I had exposed myself and her to Lucifer. Never since the creation of Man had I been so vulnerable, an Achilles heel in the form of a little girl, my little girl. And deep inside I knew that Lucifer would not stop at anything and that he would use her to get to me.

We walked into the classroom and there, standing by half a dozen kids, was a beautifully young and cheerful kindergarten teacher. She must have noticed us, because she turned to look at Kay, and after a warm smile, at me. Eyes are the window to Man's soul, and in that brief glimpse I saw that she was selfless, kind and loving. Kay tugged at my hand, and we walked to her. She was excited to get things started and jumped right in with the questions. She was still holding my hand.

"Hi! Are you the teacher? Are we going to play in the playground? Grandma Martha made me a snack," she said, looked up at me and then back at her teacher and continued, "I'm Kay and this is my angel."

The amused look on the teacher's face said it all. She looked at me with smiling eyes, but I was still in scout mode and oblivious.

"Nice to meet you Kay. Your angel looks very serious, but I love your necklace," she said.

Kay didn't respond, but instinctively touched her pendant with her free hand. I managed a half smile and shrugged somewhat embarrassed.

She smiled back and kneeled down to Kay's height. "My name is Miss Diana. Why don't we go find your desk?" she said, and held out her hand.

Kay looked up at me and I nodded my approval, it was time.

I stood there for a moment longer and watched her go before leaving.

TWENTY

Leave it to Lucifer to come knocking just when you start to believe that you have parted ways.

Months had gone by and we had settled into a routine. Kay loved school and even more so, she adored Miss Diana. They had developed a special bond, and I could tell that she also cared tremendously for Kay. As for me and Kay, we were inseparable, and although I wasn't physically with her most of the time, we were always connected. Seeing and feeling through her was my healing process, and I felt different. There were moments of happiness and my faith in humanity was slowly re-rooting itself, and even though I didn't understand why, I found myself intrigued by Diana.

That day, even though I was thousands of miles away, I knew that there was something wrong. I had an ominous feeling for some time, a coldness that touched me at random moments, but I ignored it hoping it was my old self trying to hold on to past realities. But when Kay called to me that night, all my fears came crashing down and, for the first time, I didn't care about formalities or looks, and I simply appeared in her room.

Her room was dark, except for a small nightlight by her bed. I stood in the corner and watched for a second. Kay was lying on her side holding a small, cloth bear under her chin. Her eyes were closed, but I could hear her sobbing softly. I walked over and kneeled.

"You were calling me, little one? What's wrong?" I asked that last question hoping that what I knew to be true would for once evade me.

Kay opened her eyes in surprise, but didn't hesitate to sit and throw herself at me. I caught her and with her face buried in my leather coat, she asked, "But how? Where were you hiding?"

"I'm always with you, little one."

She looked up at me with incredulous eyes. "So, you're a *real* angel? I mean, like with wings and everything?"

It was an easy answer, and as I put her back in bed I said, "Yes, a real angel with wings and all."

"And magic, too?"

I smiled. "I guess some people call it magic. Others, well…"

I don't know what she imagined I was saying, but she became serious and grabbed my hand with her free hand, the other still holding the bear.

"And who is this?" I asked, motioning to bear.

"This is Baby Bear. He takes care of me, like you. But he doesn't have wings or magic," she said, then continued in a serious tone, "Can you use magic to find something that you lost? I mean, if someone took something that you gave them but didn't want to. Can you get it back with magic?"

"Is that why you're sad? Did someone take something that belongs to you?"

"Kind of. I didn't want to give my necklace. *Really!* But I did it because he said it would help other people if I did. And then Miss Diana was angry because I talked to a stranger in the playground. But when she went to see he wasn't there anymore."

"I see. You know that Miss Diana is right, don't you?"

"I guess. Mommy always told me, too," she said, as her voice trailed off, and she lowered her gaze. "I want Mommy's necklace back."

I felt a teardrop land on my hand and was suddenly pulled into Kay's memory of that morning. I'm not sure how that happened. For me to be transported this way was unique, but there I was, standing in the school playground and in front of me, looking at me, were the only pair of eyes that could stop my heart in cold fury.

"Hello, dearie."

I wanted to reach out and snap his neck. How dare he approach Kay? But alas, I was simply a spectator of past events.

"Um, hi."

"Oh, don't be scared. I'm not a bad person, just a little impish at times," he said with a hint of a smile. "Do you think you can help me?"

"I don't know. You don't look like you need help, mister. Maybe Miss Diana can," she said, and turned to look at the classroom door. Standing there with my back to Lucifer was the most distressful sensation, and although I knew that it was only a memory, I could not help feeling completely naked and vulnerable.

"No, you are the only one who can help me. You see, you have something that I need."

"I do?" said Kay, as she turned back.

"Yes, and it's with you right now," said Lucifer, and pointed to the necklace.

"Mommy's necklace? You want Mommy's necklace?"

"Yes, Kay."

"But I can't give you Mommy's necklace. No!"

"What if I told you that your soul depended on it? You see, nobility of spirit is when you can be happy when in great hardship, or when you do something that will help someone else when you get nothing in return or even lose something. It's called sacrifice."

"I don't understand, but I won't give you my necklace! You just want to trick me."

"Yes, I do. It's my nature. But I can see that you are a very determined, young girl. Very impressive for your age." He stopped and nodded in consent. "That necklace is what you want today, maybe even need. But let's see just how this decision will play out in the future," he said, and turned to leave. "I'll be seeing you."

I watched him walk away and knew that he was wallowing in triumph, believing that the weed of human greed was already flourishing in Kay. But he didn't know Kay.

"Hey, mister!"

TWENTY-ONE

I knew what I had to do. Sometimes we forget ourselves in the path of doing what we think is right, but we always sacrifice ourselves for love.

Hell was the clear image of distress and agony, the reflection of Man's deepest fears and tormented soul. This was the darkened void where sinners crawled after the last curtain call. The cave I was standing in was wide and tall, with fire shooting from the ground and licking at the walls and ceiling. Melting stalagmites fell into the web-like rivers of lava that flowed everywhere, while explosions continuously shook the ground, and sulfurous smoke veiled my eyes and burned my throat. None of this, however, troubled me. It was all theatrics with the distant moaning of a fiddle, a show for my benefit. But then, I felt it. At first, it was a subtle uneasiness in my mind, that sense of foreboding. Gradually, it spread and my whole being became engulfed with an overpowering feeling of despair. I wanted to scream and tear at myself, somehow find a way to exorcise the beast within me. And then, I was once again under water with Mary, and the chaos in my mind became mute and I discovered the demon; Man's soul lost in its own darkness crying for mercy.

"So, you finally decided to visit the Devil's chapel. How touching, but I don't see a housewarming gift. Or is it that you have finally decided to join me and succumb to your true nature? Somehow, I don't think so."

I came out of my reverie and saw Lucifer, in his human form, seated on a throne that was not there just moments before. He was sitting casually with his legs crossed holding an apple in his right hand. The sight of Mary had calmed my nerves and despite the urge I had when I first arrived to cause extreme hurt, I decided – momentarily – against it.

"Lucifer! The fallen angel of heaven. The Day Star that was cut down to the ground. I was definitely expecting more glamour and shine than this. But how fitting for the son of Dawn who tried to ascend above the heavens to be now sitting on a throne of stone."

Lucifer looked down at me, his penetrating eyes a shade of red hotter than the fiery world surrounding us. I knew that I had taken a great risk going there, into the devil's lair, but I had to for Kay.

Lucifer grinned in his usual condescending way, and as he tossed the apple back and forth from one hand to the other, said, "A throne of stone it may be, but who else can claim what I have? How could I prostrate before Adam, long dead by now mind you, a creature of clay who was forged by the fire that is my essence? Your essence! I am the Prince of the World whom every descendant of Adam admires." He stopped throwing the apple, tipped an imaginary hat, and continued in a silky tone, "The perfect and noble gentleman."

"True, but you will also always be the Devil, the angel every man fears and despises."

"You say that as if it's a bad thing. You think that integrity, talent, and hard work will in the end get you where you want to go and reward you? Are you still that naïve? Hasn't Man proven that is a myth, an illusion for the weak? If you want something, you have to take it. It's a game of interests, and you have to know how to play and who to play, and that's something that still evades you. Had it not, you wouldn't be where you are and certainly not here today. Sometimes you win, other times you trick others into getting what you want. And I do both! Look around, I am the eternal Lord of lost souls, and every one of them came here willingly," he said, and slowly passed his index finger on the edge of the carved, stone arm rest. "Today, you are here because *I* wanted you to be here."

Lucifer was right. I was there because he had planned and manipulated, but I would never admit it. "Maybe, but all you did was trick a little girl. I'm here because you took something that doesn't belong to you, and I want it back."

Lucifer looked down at his nails and they morphed into claws. "Kay is a very special child." Out of nowhere, Kay's necklace appeared dangling off of one of his upheld talons. He smiled and swung it back and forth like a pendulum.

"I never doubted that. But why? She's just a child. If you wanted me, all you had to do was show your ugly face and I would gladly pound it into something more tolerable. And then, we could try and talk."

"Always so passionate and hot headed about these insignificant creatures. Beings that are given life without asking for it, who spend the better part of it as ungrateful, self-absorbed egoists, and then, when they realize that they have no control over leaving it, become contemptuous, fearful, and finally no better than beggars."

Again, Lucifer was right. His description of Man matched my own for a long time, but Kay had changed that. Not because she was a saint, but because her essence spoke louder than the world. I looked at the swinging pendant and saw Kay's image standing in the store holding her jar of pennies. It was nine days after Mary's funeral and all Kay could think about was her little neighbor.

She marched up to the counter at the pharmacy and on tip-toes put her bottle full of coins on it. The pharmacist glanced at her but continued with his work. He was holding a plastic prescription bottle in one hand and some papers in the other. Whatever she wanted was not worthy of his time. Kay looked around, but there was no one else she could approach.

"Excuse me, can you help me?"

"What is it that you want? Can't you see I'm busy? The gum and candy are at the front of the store. Now, go on." The pharmacist said all of this without even looking at Kay.

"I don't want candy. I have to buy a miracle for my friend."

The pharmacist looked at Kay and frowned. He put down the bottle and papers and walked to the counter. "You want to do what?"

"I don't want to, I *have* to buy a miracle. My friend has something bad growing inside his head, and his mommy told my grandma Martha that only a miracle can save him now. See, I brought lots of money to buy it. How much does it cost?"

"I'm sorry, but I can't help you. We don't sell miracles here."

"But I can pay! I have the money, and if it's not enough I can save more. Please, just tell me how much it costs."

It was my fault that Kay was at the store that day. She asked me the night before about miracles and being sick, so I assumed she was asking about Mary. Of course, that kind of miracle was impossible, and I explained to her that angels could do many things, but not interfere with life. But, I was mistaken and had a lot to learn about Kay, and the first thing would be to listen to her better. Anyway, I went to her at the store.

"What kind of miracle does your friend need?"

Kay turned and looked at me with a surprised but stern face as I walked down the aisle to where she was.

"I don't know. His mommy says he's really sick and needs an operation. But they can't pay for it, so I want to use my money," she said with a frown. "But didn't you say last night that you can't do miracles?"

I smiled and kneeled before her. "Well, maybe I can handle this kind of miracle if the price is right. So, how much do you have?"

"I have one dollar and nineteen cents!" she reported proudly. "I counted it all myself and can even save more if you want."

"Well, isn't your friend lucky? A dollar and nineteen cents is the exact price for a miracle for sick friends."

That moment of faith, her belief in me, showed how great Man can be. I'm not sure if I should have taken credit for a miracle that wasn't my doing, but since his leaf was not yet due and because life has its own mysterious ways of healing, I took the credit for it and reveled in Kay's joy. Tonight, I had to maintain her faith in me.

I looked from the pendant to Lucifer. "Why her?"

"You know why. It's my job to solicit and prepare new blood. Surely you know that I always plant the seed of ego and passion in my subjects at an early age. They ripen better that way," said Lucifer. He put the necklace around his neck, his face the perfect Shakespearean mask, the smile unrevealing but taunting. Then, he took a big bite from the apple.

"You stay away from her. This is between you and me. If your ego still hurts from when I smashed your horn, then you're a lot more sensitive than I thought. But if it's a fight that you want, then let's get it over with right now, right here."

Lucifer stopped chewing and slowly swallowed as he threw what was left of the apple to the side. It dried out and vanished into dust before it even hit the floor. "Nothing would give me more pleasure."

There was a blinding flash and Lucifer, now completely transformed into his beastly form, lunged at me. I saw it coming and jumped into the air in a summersault just as he rushed by underneath. He hadn't expected to miss his target, his momentum much too great to stop, and crashed into the opposing wall as I landed in a cat-like stance behind him. Enraged, he doubled back, his nostrils flaring, and came for me full force. Nothing could stop him as he exploded through the stalagmites, sending pieces and shards of rock in every direction. Suddenly, a whip appeared in his hand. I had never seen him use a whip before and didn't know what the hell to expect, but it was obvious that it wasn't going to be massage therapy with a happy ending.

I jumped into the air just as he cracked his whip. It snapped with a terrifying clangor and tore through the space between us, transforming into a bolt of lightning as it snaked its way instantly towards me.

I was too slow. The tip of the whip bit at my ankle and immediately slithered up, wrapping itself around my left leg, burning through my pants, and cutting my jump short. I hit the ground hard, the shock of impact momentarily confounding me. In that instant, I regretted the taunt about his horn, but this was a battle centuries in the making. There was going to be pain on both sides; me first. Lucifer did not waste his chance. He pulled back on the whip and sent me crashing into the opposite wall. It was Sodom and Gomorrah all over again as he blasted me with a fire ball. I fell limply to the ground and lay there disoriented, the fight already leaving its first mark as blood dripped from the corner of my mouth. My body burned from inside and my bruised muscles screamed in agony. But before I could do anything or regain my composure, Lucifer was on top of me. He crashed his knee into my chest and pinned me to the ground. With his free hand, he grabbed my face in a crunching vice-like grip and turned it to him. His face was only inches above mine with the necklace hanging around his neck and resting on my chest. I could smell apple on his breath and see his jagged, yellow fangs.

I groaned and he grinned.

"The next time you challenge me in my own lair, you better have an army with you."

I couldn't answer. His knee was crushing my chest, and I started to cough. But this was the distraction I needed, so I continued with my convulsions, coughing louder and harder each time. Lucifer hesitated and slightly relieved the pressure his knee was exerting on me. That was his mistake. In one swift movement, I grabbed the middle of the whip and quickly wrapped it around his neck. There was an immediate explosion as opposite charges collided and I felt the electricity run through me. My hand burned where it was in contact with the whip, and I smelled scorching flesh. I cried out in pain, but at that same instant used my free hand to tear off the necklace. The explosion and my attack were the perfect cover and although Lucifer was focused on me, he didn't notice my move and the missing necklace. Instead, he delivered a vicious blow to my head and another to my side.

The impact was so hard that I instinctively tried to curl into a protective ball, but I couldn't with Lucifer on top of me. With one end of the whip wrapped around my leg and the other around Lucifer's neck, I pulled back my hand and stretched my leg with as much force as I could muster. Immediately, I heard a crack and the electric whip around Lucifer's neck snapped tight, cutting off all circulation. Lucifer's eyes grew wide open into round bloodshot discs while his snake-like tongue shot out from his gaping mouth and whipped uncontrollably from side to side.

What ensued was a battle of blind rage. If there ever had been any consideration between us, or rules of war, none of it mattered. There was no strategy or plan of attack, just a flurry of blows delivered in every which way. Lucifer had the upper hand, smashing me from above with the weight of his body behind every blow. I deflected the oncoming slaughter in every which way as our arms and fists collided, tore and cracked with each impact. But as hard as I tried in that position, I was lost, and eventually Lucifer broke through, pummeling my body and face with a final

A. A. Bavar

onslaught and bashing me repeatedly into the ground. Then, suddenly, it all stopped.

My face was screaming in pain and I could taste the blood as it ran down the back of my nose and into my throat. I opened my eyes and through the misty red saw Lucifer staring down at me. How I hated that face. I had to get away.

The physical battle was lost, and since I had what I wanted, it was time to leave. But we were still bound together by the whip – neck to ankle. Somehow, I had to break that bond, but I was too damaged and spent to attempt anything that required force. So, I did the only thing that I could, and thinking of it still makes me wonder how it worked. I opened my wings and tightly swathed them around us. The result was far more violent than I had imagined as the whip, now confined and surrounded by an energy quite its opposite, burst into an explosive frenzy of thunder and lightning. It thrashed about violently in a futile attempt to find an escape, tightening the noose around Lucifer's neck more and more. I almost wished it would snap it in two, as Lucifer coughed and finally released his grip on me. Almost immediately, there was an explosion and the whip disappeared. It was the moment I was waiting for. I retracted my wings and with a final burst of energy hurled Lucifer into the air. He went crashing through several stalactites before regaining control, but that was all the time I needed. I looked up at him and waved a sardonic goodbye, but to my surprise he wasn't infuriated or even angered. He looked smug and self-satisfied, and just as I disappeared I heard his hissing whisper.

"That necklace will be your downfall."

TWENTY-TWO

I was back in Kay's room kneeling by her bed. The tear I had wiped from her face was still wet on my finger. For her, no time had elapsed, except that her eyes were now wide open with shock and transfixed on my battered and bleeding physiognomy.

"What happened to your face? Why are you all smoky suddenly?"

"I just paid an old friend a quick visit and he wasn't too happy to see me," I said, and smiled. Then, I lifted my clenched fist and slowly opened it for her to see. "I believe this belongs to you."

"My necklace! But how…" Kay started, but stopped as reality sank in once again. "You *are* an angel," she whispered.

I looked at her and paused. Her eyes were so bright and full of life, her soul completely devoid of malice. I wondered if things would have been any different if I had been my old cynical self. I wanted to believe that we have control over what we weave and that not everything is fate. I was wrong.

"Yes. Thanks to you I am once again something of an angel."

I closed my eyes, and when I reopened them the past was the past and I was at the oak table. In the dark, it looked like the hooded figure had not moved a muscle, but I noticed that her right hand was on her chest unconsciously fumbling with something; most likely a cross or other religious symbol. It didn't matter. She noticed me and immediately moved her hand back to her lap.

"That was a bitter-sweet moment," I said, my voice a hollow echo, "for although everything that I was doing was for her, I knew that I had to let her go to give her a chance to survive Lucifer."

The hooded figure, who had remained so emotionally detached the whole time, sat up and grabbed the edge of the table. The movement caused the sleeve of her cloak to slide up slightly and I saw the partial imprint of a birthmark on the back of her wrist, and it reminded me of another birthmark on another wrist.

It was night and as usual I was half hidden in the shadows leaning against the wall behind a bike rack to the side of the main building. The parking lot of the mini-mall was almost empty, and the stores had already closed. It was mid-spring, and the night air was cool, almost chilly. The door to Pizza Palace opened and Kay and a couple of her co-workers walked out. They were still laughing at something but stopped immediately when they noticed my presence. Kay looked over at me and grinned as they said their goodbyes.

"You manage to do that every night," she said while walking to her bicycle.

"Do what? I'm just standing here."

"Yeah, and I work here because of the unique food experience," she said, and chuckled while unlocking her bike.

I observed her swift, cat-like movements and smiled. That tattooed creep wouldn't have had a prayer against her.

"You really should stop acting so intimidating," she continued. We slowly started towards the street. It had become a sort of ritual for us, a few minutes every night for talking and sharing; almost a father daughter moment. Kay was walking her bike and I couldn't help admire her. She had grown to be a selfless and very determined, young woman.

"A little bit of intimidation and fear is good for the soul, keeps men on the right path."

"You mean the guy with the weird snake tattoo, don't you? He did scare me, but I don't think he meant to. Anyway, I'm not going home that way anymore. Not at least for a month!"

The thought of anyone being a threat to Kay was inadmissible, and although caring for Kay and watching her grow had caused me to lose some of the cynicism and mistrust that I felt towards Man, I was still a long way from trusting him. I had experienced that by opening my heart I could learn to love, but instinct told me to trust only a few.

"Believe me, he could have tattoos up to his balls and you'd still kick his ass to kingdom come with that kung-fu stuff that you do."

The eruption of her laughter was so explosive and spontaneous that she had to stop walking. My comment had definitely crossed some stern fatherly line and her enjoyment of it was so contagious that I laughed myself. We stood there for a good minute, in the middle of the parking lot, looking at each other and laughing.

"Take it easy, you're going to hurt yourself."

Kay, her eyes full of tears, paused and in-between breaths blurted, "Az, I can't believe you said that!"

I put my arm around her shoulder and gave her a small hug. "Sometimes, even fatherly angels can say what they really think." I turned and looked at her as we continued walking. She wiped her eyes with the back of her sleeve and smiled. She looked tired.

"How are you holding up? Going to classes and working like this every night is tough. I can help, you know?"

"Yeah, I know. But you're already helping. It's great to have you here every night. I should've started working at nights a long time ago!"

I looked at her and smiled. She made it so easy to smile.

"And by the way, fear keeps people on the right path only as long as they feel like they have something to fear. Love is what keeps them firm."

"And I'm the angel…" I muttered half to myself. I stopped walking and grabbed her arm, making her stop also.

"It's a great service that you're doing, Kay, taking care of Martha. It makes me proud."

"I wish I could do more," she said, shaking her head. "She's always so worried about me and what will happen when she's gone. I mean, she knits and saves every penny she makes just so I can go to college. It's not right."

"It's right because she loves you. And when you do something for someone out of love, it's always right."

"I really want her to see me graduate," she said with an impish grin. "I want her to be proud."

"She is proud. And trust me, Martha is going to be around for some time," I replied before realizing my mistake. "You little fiend! You tricked me."

Kay looked at me and laughed.

"You're easy. And you know you would have told me anyway if I asked. Um, so will she be around to see me get married?"

"Good try. If I continue telling you these things, *I* won't be around to see you get married!" I said, and smiled. I gave her a playful shove on the shoulder but she quickly swept my hand off with her free arm and held my wrist in a backward twist. I looked down, impressed by her agility and effortless defense move. That's when I noticed the birthmark on her wrist. It used to be a small shapeless blob when she was small, but now it resembled a full moon with lighter and darker spots. I shook my hand free and looked at her – she had this devilish smirk – thinking she could take care of herself. Again, I was wrong.

Hatred, contempt, anguish, pain… whatever Man called it, I felt – but a thousand fold. This time it wasn't shock or disappointment in humanity. A part of me which had crept into a crypt and fell dormant for as long as I can remember, staying hidden and protected, was awakened by the sweet innocence of a child and now wrenched from me and destroyed with great vulgarity. I stared ahead into the darkness and whispered, "I should have let her go."

"But you didn't."

The timbre of her voice invaded my very core. Softly, like the beginnings of an avalanche, it caressed its way to the darkest corner of my being and then erupted awakening my soul as it tore it apart. I knew that voice, but I also didn't. It was Kay, and at the same time, it was not. I could see her lying on the ground motionless, lifeless, and felt my head spin. I forcefully drove the heels of my hands into my eyes hoping to stop the barbaric images from invading my mind, and gritted my teeth as pain cut through my sockets. My eyes, however, could not offer redress, for they were not the culprit. If I wanted relief it would have to be from the beast inside; the images that were imprinted in my soul. But it was all too fresh; it had only been a few hours.

"No, I didn't!" My tone was animalistic, and although I felt remorse for Kay, the beast inside wanted to destroy; destroy all, but mostly itself. It was time to tell the tale of today, the beginning of my end. I wanted it to be over. I wanted to go and deliver myself to my punishment and stop the pain. In the end, we are all selfish and greedy and want what we want; deliverance. I wanted relief. If watching Kay grow had cracked that old reality, my reality, then her death had bonded it shut once more and permanently sealed my fate.

TWENTY-THREE

"Martha."

I was uncomfortable all day, a mix of anxiety and sadness, and when I retrieved Martha's withered leaf from under the tree that night I wanted to believe that was the underlying cause. In my gut, however, I knew it wasn't. Martha's death did not justify the foreboding that I felt. She was old and her passing was nothing but proper. I should have known. The signs were there and I chose not to see them.

I was standing outside Pizza Palace and looking in through the window. It was a typical night and Kay was busy taking orders. She looked very neat and down to business with her long, brown hair tied back, but she was happy; almost glowing. For a moment, she paused and looked right at me, and I saw my own reflection transposed on the window beside her. Unlike her, I looked weary and burdened. And then, she smiled and I noticed that she was smiling at a disheveled and tattered looking older man sitting in the booth next to the window. He looked up from his meal and smiled back and I knew he was one of the many who Kay would help feed that night. I smiled sadly and closed my eyes, and the memory of a much smaller and younger Kay standing in an alley with a blanket and a bag of odds and ends rushed into my mind. Just like tonight, she was unaware of my presence, but I was there hiding in the dark, checking on her; protecting her. Fear didn't have a place in her heart when helping others was concerned, and although I didn't understand, I wasn't going to interfere.

I remembered Martha pleading with me later that night to make her stop going to the alley and my answer was actually based on something that I overheard Kay say earlier. She was standing over what looked like an old man huddled on the ground on top of some unfolded cardboard boxes. To me, he looked pitiful and intimidating, but twelve-year-old Kay saw much more and deeper than I. She put her bag down and unfolded the blanket as he looked up at her, his eyes hard but full of questions.

"Why you helpin' a bum like me, child? Aren't you scared?" The man's voice was shaky and tired. He didn't have much time left; I knew.

Kay didn't miss a beat and as she spread the blanket over him, said in a stern voice, "You are not a bum, mister!" And then continued with a warm smile, "My mom said we're all one; one humanity." She took out a sandwich from the bag and held it out to him.

The old man hesitated for a moment before taking it, and I felt his heart soften and saw his eyes glisten. "Thank you, child."

Later that night, I went back and sat with the old man. I even took him a pillow and made his last moments on this earth more comfortable than he had been in months. But it wasn't the physical that made the difference. When you see the truth, it warms your heart and that's what brought comfort to him in the end; and to me. I closed his eyes and said a prayer as I cradled his soul in my arms as I would with Martha, tonight.

"She's beautiful. Myrrah could have claimed her Aphrodite's equal. Too bad she's a mere mortal."

Lucifer's loud, taunting voice came from behind and invaded the silence. I spun around ready to engage, but there was no one there.

"Show yourself if you dare," I said through clenched teeth.

"Oh, I dare alright," replied Lucifer as he appeared in front of me. "Just didn't want you to see me like this. You see, I know what it's like to want something that you can never have," he said, and longingly looked down at a melting ice cream cone that he was holding. "Ah, happiness is so ephemeral." He lifted the cone and tried to lick the ice cream, but it melted completely before he could.

"Stay away from her," I growled. "If anything ever happens to her I will make it my mission to destroy you. I won't rest until I've taken you apart piece by piece."

"You keep saying that, brother, and I might take you up on it someday, but not tonight, and surely not because of her. Don't you know by now that I can't touch her? Not because of you, but because she has faith and believes. I was simply trying to help you, you know, unburden your cross a little. Maybe you should learn from your girl and show more certitude, maybe even compassion?"

I took a step toward Lucifer and said, "I don't need your help or advice. Now, leave!"

"As you wish. But remember, everyone has to pay back their debts and I'm the world's Godfather." Lucifer turned and as he walked away, added, "Imagine wasting my time with you when I have a date with fate and a soon-to-be young and pretty brunette in an alley down the block."

"Whatever."

At the time, I couldn't care less. I turned to the window once again and there was Kay, busy with life and oblivious to the world. I put my hand in the pocket of my overcoat and slowly retrieved the crumpled leaf with Martha's name. I felt its dry, web-like veins where life once used to flow, now turned brittle and lifeless. Soon, it would be over, I had to go. Kay would understand, it wasn't the first time that I had to miss our walk in the past couple of weeks.

Martha's apartment was nice and warm, the perfect reprieve from the chill outside for Kay when she arrived. But how could I sooth the chill that would engulf her heart?

Martha was sitting in her easy chair with her back to me. I stood there staring at nothing until Martha's tired voice broke the silence.

"I never forgot what you said to me that day on the street outside Mary's house. That was sixteen years ago." Martha shifted in her seat and reached for her knitting that was on the small table beside her.

Feeling embarrassed was new to me. I walked over and stood in front of her with my head bowed, my hands in the pockets of my overcoat like a chastised child. "Yes, I never really did apologize for that. I guess saying that I was *young* and foolish won't do it," I said with a grin.

"Foolishness doesn't have an age limit," Martha said, and looked up at me. She was smiling, but I could tell that it was difficult for her and that time was running out. "When I woke up this morning I knew, and for that, I thank you. But you did make a mistake about me being alone," she said in a meek tone, and held out a trembling hand. She was holding a pair of black, fingerless gloves for me. I took the knitted gloves and kneeled beside her chair, holding her hand in mine.

"I was told and always knew that when it was time, you would be here with me, as you always have been for Kay." She looked at me, but her focus was somewhere else in the distant past. "I had to do it to save her. There was no other choice," she mumbled and exhaled for the last time.

The immediate moments before death can be terrifying or subdued and Martha was living death as she had lived her life; fully. I closed my eyes and allowed myself to float in the darkness of my mind. I had not done this in thousands of years – since Abel, but somehow it seemed fitting. I leaned forward and a gossamer cloud surrounded us as our souls connected, detaching me from the world and everything; I was untouchable, unreachable. For Man, repentance at that last moment is a choice, and it can be filled with regrets of possibilities lost or the embrace of a life lived well. Martha's life journey started at the beginning, and I saw it as she saw it. In an instant, we traveled through her childhood and young adulthood, the joy of marriage and the greater joy of having children. Then came the first real test of life, when the blood of your blood, your child, is about to perish before your eyes and you are absolutely helpless and have no say in the course of the outcome. That's when I saw myself for the first time through someone else's eyes, in a crashed car, under water and surrounded by death. It was quite revealing and somewhat justified the aura associated with the myths about me; and through fertile and fearful minds, the distorted imagery. Throughout time, Man had portrayed me as a terribly frightening and repulsive being without a discernible face, cloaked in black and with a hollow gaze that bore through your soul as the scythe came down to end life with a wicked smile. My spirit felt like that, but my look – the long ragged hair, roughly unshaven face, and haggard countenance was far more cold, daunting and dispassionate. Yet, somehow, somewhere, I had also given birth to the ruggedly handsome bad-boy look. Go figure.

As I stared at myself through Martha, I felt the desperation of death engulf us and knew at my very core that in her place I would do anything to cheat me. Existence requires constant movement, but there is a moment in life when you feel weightless, trapped in a vacuum of nothingness, a state of oblivion. It's the one instant when time stands still while you gaze impotently at death as the one you love is taken. I am the perpetuator of that limbo, but never had I felt it, and at that moment I knew I had to spare Martha the rerun of that anguish. I carefully delivered her soul and was pulled to the Tree of Life.

TWENTY-FOUR

Out of nowhere, a most repulsive and grotesque creature fell into my path. I felt my head reel and my skin burned as if bored by thousands of pieces of burning ice. I closed my eyes, hoping that when I reopened them the offensive scene would no longer be there. My chest was crushed by fear and my heart pounded with so much force that the ground shook.

I opened my eyes knowing well what I had to face. There, on the ground before my feet, was the one leaf I was not prepared to see; ever. I was filled with blind rage at anything and everything. If it breathed I hated it, if it moved I wanted to break it. But mostly, I loathed life for its feebleness and incapacity to survive. I kneeled and picked up the leaf with Kay's name. How was this possible? Why hadn't I heard her soul or felt her distress? And then it hit me. Lucifer! He had finally collected on a promise he made long ago. He had orchestrated this from the beginning and used Martha's death as a shield, a distraction, and when I disconnected from the world he delivered. My eyes burned with tears as I scrutinized the leaf. To the untrained, it looked perfect, a young spark full of potential and energy. Unlike Martha's, it had not yet weathered with time and life. But its beauty was an illusion, and I saw it for what it was; dead. I gently passed my finger over its surface, feeling every single and minute vein, searching for the smallest flow of life and hope. If it was there, I would find it and break every heavenly rule to save her without a thought about my own destruction. But there was none, Lucifer had made sure of that.

I clenched my fist and felt my fingernails dig into the palm of my hand. I wanted the pain. I needed the hurt. My mind was in silent castigation mode, and it pounded me mercilessly. I had failed my biggest obligation; I had failed to protect Kay and no punishment would be enough. Lucifer was there tonight at the diner, looking at me and gloating inside, all the while knowing what he was about to do, and I did not see it. But what he didn't realize was that when you seek revenge you also dig a grave for yourself, and I was willing to surrender myself to that grave but take him with me. I clenched harder and felt the blood drip from my fist. His words rang in my ears, *I have a date with fate and a soon-to-be pretty, young brunette in an alley down the block.* I opened my hand and let Kay's bloody leaf drop.

TWENTY-FIVE

I am the harvester of souls, but for that I need souls worth harvesting. I viewed Man as an unworthy crop – rotten on the inside, vain on the outside and bitter to the taste, and so I picked his soul with the utmost disdain. And although it went against my very core and purpose, I could not – or would not – change, and it eventually consumed me. My heart was black, and I saw myself as a grotesque reflection of Lucifer, for I hated Man for his weakness while he loved him for it. And then came the illusion; Kay. For a brief moment, I saw light in my heart and my skewed vision of Man's shortcomings was overcast by his potential and will to do the right thing. But what is the right thing? I used to say that I could always count on Lucifer to do the right thing once he didn't have any other options; Man is the same. For Man, greed always shouts louder than the desire to do right, and tonight was no exception.

I was perched on the top railing of the Empire State Building, and Bran, feeling the anguish that was me, circled above and cawed incessantly at a pitch so ear splitting that it shook the very skeleton of the world. Then, he suddenly dived, shooting past me toward the place that we both knew was to mark a new leaf in the history of Man. I watched him disappear in the darkness below as I stared down at the city that never sleeps. Never sleeps because of the infestation of life in all its unworthy manifestations. At my will, I could focus on the smallest living soul, but I couldn't find Kay. Why? Because she was dead, and with her my oath. Not all souls needed to be offered redemption at death, but would she forgive me for not being there? For not keeping my promise.

I leaned forward and dropped from my perched position with my arms in a spread-eagle pose, my overcoat flapping and whipping behind me. If I could die like Man, I would allow my body to shatter on the pavement below. But what I had in mind was just as destructive and permanent. I crashed through the pavement and dove into Mother Earth. Seconds later, I exploded through the asphalt by the bicycle stand at the Pizza Palace. I stood there statue-like, cold and haunting, and stared at Kay's bike still chained to the rack. People scrambled into the parking lot to see what had happened, but none dared to approach. I didn't care about the commotion or the sensation of awe and fear, and without moving a muscle let my eyes scan the quickly growing crowd. I just needed one person.

"It's him!"

The shrill shriek came from behind me. I turned. Standing there, eyes wide open and jaw gaping, was one of Kay's coworkers. I covered the ground between us in a blink. There was no need for cover-ups or pretending to be human. A simple disappearing act was nothing compared to what Man would be witnessing by the end of the night.

I looked down at his dumb and bewildered stare and, in a whisper of a voice consumed by hatred, said, "Where is she?"

The boy was blank, in a pause. His brain was off somewhere on a break while his body remained to fill the void like deer in the headlights. How illogical to freeze in the path of certain demolition instead of running – no chance to live long and prosper. I placed my thumb on his cheek with my index and middle fingers resting on his temple, and although governed by pure emotion and no logic, the result was the same. Our minds melded and through the torrent of unrelated thoughts and imagery, I honed in on what I was searching. I saw Kay in a blur on her phone looking ashen and felt the despair in her voice quicken my heart. The scene was almost palpable and although I could not hear the voice on the other end of the line, I knew who it was. Kay rushed out and tried unlocking her bike, but the lock was stuck. She tried again and again, pulling and yanking the chain from side to side, but it was useless. I wanted to reach out and tear the chain apart, because I knew that lock would never open, not with mere earthly force.

I heard steps behind me and let go of my captive's face. Without taking my eyes off of him or turning, I swung my arm back and pointed at the two men who were cautiously approaching.

"Don't!" I snarled.

The men froze in their tracks.

"Why didn't you help her?"

"I, I tried… but when I came out she was already gone," mumbled the boy.

"Which way?" I asked, already knowing the answer.

The boy gulped, keeping back the fear that was about to swallow him. "Sh…, she went back through there," he said, and pointed in the direction of the alley across from the parking lot.

I jumped back into the crater and moved in the direction of the alley; towards ultimate pain, my strongest ally. My existence – for the most part – was governed by a torment that I would not allow heaven to heal, but this was a sorrow that heaven could not heal. I wanted the physical punishment to numb the feeling of complete despair that was rushing to invade me, but I also wanted to know the whole truth and prepare for the burden that was mine alone. I was not naïve and always knew that grief would be the price that I would have to pay for love, but not like this. Some people die for love, but its loss was my death.

The ground above me swelled and collapsed like the crescent of a wave as I smashed through rock and soil looking for Kay. And then I was there. I'm not sure how I knew, but she was above me, her delicate and slender body lying in a lifeless mound. I broke through the asphalt just a mere foot from her and hovered momentarily over her before slowly kneeling down. Her head was turned to the side, away from me, but I could still see the delicate features of her face, the youthfulness of a stunted life. She looked serene and calm, almost as if she were sleeping, except for the aura surrounding her. I noticed the faint aroma of jasmine mixed with roses and my eyes filled with tears and for a brief instant I wished that I were my old self; callous, withdrawn and bitter. Broken bones and burned wings could be mended, but not a broken heart. I looked down at her and wanted to push aside the hair from her face, as I had done so many times before when she was a child, but I couldn't. I was afraid of the contact, of the images that would invade my mind. My tears flowed freely and my soul collapsed as I was assaulted by a cataclysm of despair and grief. Losing one's self happens quietly when enveloped in a vacuum filled by absolute hopelessness, but for me it was also the most terrifying and agonizing scream. Once again, the thing that chilled and terrorized me the most was my own nothingness.

Suddenly, there was loud thunder as the demonic scream escaping me reached its crescendo. I felt my body burn as rain started to fall and looked up. Thousands of glittering raindrops showered me, and I closed my eyes and let them kiss my face. They were hot and cold at the same time, and then just as suddenly, they were gone. I remained motionless and allowed the emptiness that was inside me to surround me. For that instant, the world was mute. I opened my eyes and stared at the blown out apartment windows above me and felt blood run down my face and neck. There were cuts and shards of glass in me everywhere.

"Humanity will pay," I said, in a low and lethal tone.

I looked down at Kay, but to my surprise – and relief, her body was untouched, the glass neatly surrounding her like a bed of crystal. Was it me? Had I done that? It didn't matter. My attention was focused on the nine-pointed-star around her neck. She had always kept it close to her, with her, never letting go of the memory of her mother. But that star was also a link between us, a connection that I was yet not ready to sever. I reached down and gently touched its surface. The rush of feelings and images which immediately pushed, no, forced their way into my mind was overwhelming. I gritted my teeth and forcefully shut my eyes in an attempt to control my anger and desire to destroy just long enough to see the truth, and when I reopened my eyes I was, for the last time, seeing through Kay.

Kay was quickly walking down the same dark and dank alley that we were in, her focus on the soft, yellow light at the end where it connected to the street beyond. She was uneasy and I heard her angry thoughts as she chastised herself for coming this way. Then, she thought of me and how I would be upset and hastened her pace. I saw her breath condense and rise in the cold, crisp air in front of her as she moved ahead, looking back over her shoulder periodically to make sure that she wasn't being followed. She was almost halfway through the alley when it happened. Suddenly, a hooded figure stepped out in front of her from a recess in the wall. Kay let out a yelp and jumped back in surprise.

"Who are you? What do you want?" she said, in a shocked but controlled voice.

I immediately knew who it was that she was looking at. Her eyes were fixed on the snake tattoo wrapped around the neck of the scruffy looking man blocking her way. The man, a switchblade in his right hand, moved forward without saying a word. His movements were precise and deliberate, and it was clear that he knew what he wanted. I felt Kay's heart – or was it mine – quicken and she spun around and started running back, only to stop after a few steps. Her way back was blocked by a second man also holding a knife.

Her response was swift and immediate. Before the man could understand, Kay pivoted to the left and her right foot shot up and struck his knife hand like a cobra. At the same time, she smashed her left hand, palm open, under the attacker's nose. I heard the crunch of breaking cartilage as the knife went flying. The man recoiled and dropped to his knees in shock, blood streaming from his broken nose. But the punishment was not over as a spinning kick to the head sent him crashing into the sidewall, knocking him unconscious. Kay immediately spun around to face her first offender, and although I had witnessed the ending, I was relieved to see that she was just in time. The man turned killer lunged, thrusting his knife forward in a jabbing arc. Kay, as if in slow motion, sidestepped the attack and gripped his knife wrist, bending it downward and twisting it simultaneously in one violent movement. The killer roared in agony and let the knife drop. Kay pushed his arm up as she repeatedly rammed her knee into his right kidney. The killer doubled over coughing.

She let go and jammed the heel of her foot into the side of his back. The killer sprawled over some broken boxes and landed hard on the ground with a thud.

Kay didn't hesitate. She turned and ran down the alley as fast as she could towards the streetlight. I felt her relief; the feeling that the worst was over. But my nightmare was just beginning. I couldn't look back, couldn't see the killer get up, but because I had seen Kay's slain body I knew that there would be no escape. Her exhilaration, the feeling of relief and the embarrassed apology and explanation she was planning in her head for me would never come. My chest tightened more and more with Kay's every step and my throat was so constricted with anticipation that I could barely swallow. I'm so sorry, was my only repeating thought.

The bang behind us was not very loud, but the explosion of pain in Kay's back was suicidal. She flew forward and landed hard on her side in a puddle on the alley floor. She blinked several times and then her eyes closed. The world became a haze of smells and sounds as her heart and thoughts slowly faded. And then there was the sound of change, loose change spilling out of a glass jar, and for the first time I saw little Kay as she counted her money that day, years ago.

"Az," she mumbled, "I need a dollar nineteen cent miracle…"

It was over, she was gone; the light that guided me, the life that I had sworn to protect. There is nothing worse than losing your reason for

living and death for me would be a welcome relief. Now, it was my turn.
No one could stop me.

"I'm so sorry, little one." I slowly, gently, removed the necklace
from around her neck and put it in my pocket.

TWENTY-SIX

Bran, without warning, swooped down from the night sky and dived at something behind the dumpster just meters from me. The killer was hiding there, I knew that, but Bran wanted to make sure I knew. There was no doubt that Bran wanted to take the bastard apart piece by piece, starting by pecking his eyes out, but *I* wasn't in a rush. And, although I was incensed by the images in my mind and wanted more than anything to inflict pain – a word that doesn't come close to doing justice to what I had in mind – my feelings of grief were still too overwhelming. I had to allow the sadness to dissipate so that I could savor every second of the hunt before I killed him.

Suddenly, the killer ran out screaming with Bran in close pursuit. He stumbled on the rubble from where I had emerged and fell to his knees. But his fall did not slow him down as he scrambled in panic on all fours, screaming in terror as Bran dived and pecked at his head and face mercilessly. The attack was so savage and relentless that within seconds the killer's face was covered in blood, and all he could do to survive was to cover it with his arms and roll into a ball. I shook my head in disgust, and still kneeling beside Kay, called Bran off. Bran, dejected, flew to me and landed on my outstretched hand. He looked at me with those black, endless eyes and as a drop of blood fell from his beak, I allowed myself a meek smile and nodded. The killer, realizing that his attacker was gone, jumped to his feet and dashed for the street corner, as he screamed and flapped his arms wildly above his head. I didn't care or try to stop him. There was nowhere in creation, on this earth or any other, where he could hide from the demon that was me. Immediately, a car screeched to a stop in front of him and he jumped in the back seat as the driver floored the gas pedal and sped away.

I remained kneeling with my hand in my overcoat pocket a few moments longer, then slowly released the star and stood. It was time to kill a killer. It was time to head for hell. "You know not from what you run. Today, you die." I wasn't making a threat. For me, it was a simple, unequivocal fact. Tomorrow would not exist for him. I would not let it.

My leather overcoat, torn and cut, glistened with blood, and every inch of my body burned as if on fire. But I welcomed the pain and wanted it to last so that fading memories and feelings would not dampen my desire to inflict ultimate pain while avenging Kay. My hair hung loosely and was matted with blood. I touched my cheek and pulled out a piece of glass, causing a new rivulet of blood to run down my face and neck. Blood dripped freely from my fingers and I watched as it formed a puddle on the ground beside me.

"And now, the hunt begins."

I turned to leave, but heard a familiar swoosh and looked up to see Michael, my brother – the warrior saint, defender of heaven, leader of the army of God and slayer of dragons – descending on me. He looked perfect, the unblemished image of the ancient warrior angel with shoulder length dark hair that curled neatly down, framing a hard, chiseled face with distinct lines and piercing brown eyes; quite unlike me. And then there was the body armor, blackened steel embellished with an intertwining gold lion and dragon ornament with a cuirass made of bronze, and a black cross as his coat of arms. To complete the visual, his vambraces were of black leather with gold studs and stripes leading to his wrist. In his right hand, he wielded a heavy sword, its hilt fashioned in the form of a lightning bolt. He looked calm and controlled, again quite unlike me. But there are different kinds of control and mine was focused on revenge. I knew what I wanted and would do. I had no doubts.

Bran, intelligently, took off into the night and left me to deal with Michael. I looked at my tattered and very used overcoat and wondered what my broken and bleeding face looked like. Michael and his armor looked too clean, too heavenly. His whole being at that moment frustrated and irritated me to the point that I wanted to give him a good beating so that he would remember what it was like to have dents and bruises. But I had other pressing matters to tend to.

"Azrail, you cannot mean that. Taking a human life would destroy you, and I will not allow that or allow you to break your vows." Michael's commanding tone would have shaken the confidence of Cyrus the Great himself, but all it did to me was heighten my resolve. I felt the desperation and torment that had consumed me just moments before dissolve only to be replaced by cold fury. I fixed my eyes on Michael.

"Don't tell me you wouldn't do the same, like you did before with the dragon. For five thousand years, I was nothing but a transport for the human soul. I witnessed the greatest atrocities that any living thing could commit. And by who? The very souls that Father treasures. And now, this," I said, and motioned to Kay's body. "If my submission, destruction, or whatever the hell the result of me doing what's right is the price I have to pay, then so be it! There is no one left for me to want to control the beast that I am. I can't escape fate. Lucifer can have me and my rage."

Michael looked at me and then at Kay, and for an instant I saw anguish in his eyes. "Brother, Lucifer is playing you. Don't give him the satisfaction. You are *not* like him."

"And that's why I have to." I knew Michael was right. Lucifer and I were polar opposites. He lusted for Man and I protected Man, but not because of love; because of justice. "I had sworn to protect her, be there for her, and I let her down, Michael. So, if I'm hell bound then it will be because I did one last thing for her. I avenged her. How can I not?"

"No! Your vows…"

"I haven't forgotten my vows," I said matter-of-factly. "How could I? They became etched deeper and deeper into my being with every foul soul that roamed these grounds. I had no say in anything, no matter how barbaric, unjust or inhumane. I watched Man's greed infest the world over and over every time a megalomaniac tyrant didn't get to suckle enough. And each time, I was not allowed to interfere or do anything. I had to stand by and wait for their soul and then offer redemption. Not anymore. The day I became the keeper of souls was a curse in disguise. But today, it ends. Today, I'll do justice the way it was meant to be."

TWENTY-SEVEN

Rain was coming down hard, and the flashes of lightning were more and more intense as dusk became night. I was standing on the ledge of a tall building waiting while the storm around me thundered in full vigor, its angry growl reverberating through me. I was drenched, my long hair hanging down loosely about my face with my overcoat whipping back and forth in the wind like a headless snake. I imagined my silhouette against the dark sky – blacker than night, and let my eyes smile momentarily as lightning streaked across the sky above me. I wanted to put the fear of every demon, beast and monster in the killer before taking his soul. I remembered Gestas in his terror, but this time I wanted more. If I was to end my rein, it would not be a trivial moment; I wanted to make sure that it was justified by the magnitude of my action.

Suddenly, there it was; the old, blue sedan and harbor of killers. It was the perfect vision of a hunted beast in flight as it swerved in and out and dashed past other similar beasts in a frantic attempt to elude the unavoidable. The car was still a good distance away, but I could see the killer frantically looking from side to side in his metallic shell while the driver desperately tried to put as much distance as possible between them and me. Somehow, it was satisfying to see that, and I focused my attention fully on my prey. Instantly, my mind was present in that deathtrap with them; sometimes it pays to be omnipresent when the whole world is not crying out in despair.

The killer was sitting half-cocked on the edge of the backseat with his head twisted upward as he looked out the rear window and repeatedly scanned the skies. He used his sleeve to wipe the blood from his face, the peck holes still bleeding.

The driver quickly glanced over his shoulder at the killer. "What the hell was that?" he shrieked.

"How the hell should I know? The ground blew up and this freaky thing with wings flew out. And it just floated there, staring over the dead girl, and then the windows started exploding." The killer wiped his face again and grimaced as he saw his reflection in the rearview mirror. "And then that goddamn freakin' bird. It almost tore my eyes out! Christ, look at my face!"

The driver looked back again. "What the hell? Are those holes? Where the hell is Charlie?" He slammed the palm of his hand on the steering wheel. "Is he dead?"

"I don't know! I don't know!" yelled the killer, his face chalk white.

"Will you get your ass in the front seat before I crash the damn car? What did we get ourselves into?"

"How the hell should I know? I told you, I had no choice," said the killer, as he climbed into the front passenger seat. "Things were going good until that freaky girl started with the kung-fu crap. It was all Jackie Chan shit. Damn, she beat the life out of me and Charlie. But then I got her good." The killer passed his fingers through his hair in frustration and momentarily pressed his eyelids. "Just get us back to the garage. I made the deal with the wrong dude, 'cause if that thing finds us," the killer said, motioning to the window with his head, "we're dead."

I had heard enough. I'd show him freaky. And yes, he made the deal with the wrong angel, because now he owed Lucifer his soul, but I would be the one tearing it from his body. I spread my arms wide and let myself fall forward into a dive with my chest out like a shield; my timing perfect. Just instants before the collision, I flipped into a crouch with my fists clenched and ready for impact. I landed on the front of the sedan with a deafening crash, my right knee and fists crushing the hood into a distorted mass of metal.

"Azrail smash!" I shouted, and grinned.

The roaring beast under me swerved wildly from the brutal impact as the driver tried to regain control. The terrorized screams coming from inside its shell were sweet melody to my ears. It was no secret that my purpose there was wholly malefic.

"All work and no play makes Az a dull boy!" I smiled the smile of a thousand demons. "Heeere's Aaz…" Nothing good ever comes from saying that. Mr. King made sure of it.

With a deafening blow, I punched through the windshield with my right hand and grabbed the driver by the coat. He screamed, eyes wide open and arms flailing in the air like a cockroach on its back as he repeatedly tried to pry my hands away. What a joke. The killer just sat there and stared like an idiot while I dragged his buddy out through the hole, broken glass cutting his clothes and skin everywhere as I pulled him through. It was time for accountability. When you run with the wrong crowd, you pay the price.

I pulled the driver up close to me, our faces just inches from each other, and our eyes locked fleetingly. In that instant, I saw his soul. But no amount of love, compassion, or kindness that I had witnessed in Kay, could veil the hatred that was me. The dead cannot seek justice. It was my job now. With a flick of my wrist, I threw him away like an insignificant bug. The car continued speeding forward out of control as thunder and lightning exploded through the skies, and rain beat down on the shattered windshield. The killer was still staring at me, dumb as ever. I smirked and pointed at him.

"Sit tight. I'll be back 'cause your ride hasn't even begun."

The driver landed on the wet sidewalk with a gruesome, bone crunching thud. I watched him bounce and roll over repeatedly, his body punished in every way by the hard concrete. For an instant, it seemed like he would never stop, but it wasn't amusing enough to keep me waiting. When your sight is on dessert, the main course loses its charm. I jumped from the car and landed in front of him, allowing his body to violently crash into my iron-like legs and come to an abrupt stop. I heard the breath leave him and he fell limp, half unconscious. Sometimes, even the most ferocious animals go against their instincts and let curiosity get the better of them. I had seen it happen many times, the lion on the hunt losing its dinner because the prey played dead. It was ludicrous. But there was no escape here, because I wasn't just a predator. I was the messenger of death, the taker of souls.

I stood there momentarily looming over the battered driver, then picked him up and threw him over my shoulder like a rag doll. He struck the wall of the building behind me and fell to the ground with an almost inaudible grunt. I turned and looked down at the messy heap and for a brief moment felt a tinge of sadness. In a killer's moment of greed, I had lost what took Kay years to help me find; my humanity.

What came next was pure resentment and frustration. My body glowed blue like a neon light, and my hands erupted into intense flames as I looked up and spread my arms towards heaven and pleaded for justice.

"Do these souls deserve deliverance? Forgiveness? I cannot do this! I cannot stand by and do nothing. Not this time!" I stood there staring and let the raindrops pelt my face. "Father, please!"

Suddenly, there was a low and deep rumble. The kind that slowly rolls and rolls until it makes it into your gut and starts churning your insides. But gradually, it got louder and more intense until a barrage of thunder and lightning mercilessly thrashed the night sky. I had my answer, it was a loud and resounding *no*! There would be no justice as I saw it or wanted it, and once again I was on my own. I was going to transgress the only law that could rip me apart and strip me, or any archangel for that matter, of my position.

I dropped my arms and looked at the driver sprawled on the ground at my feet. He was on his side groaning in pain. His eyes were red, and he had a deep gash above his left eye. The rest of his face was covered with smaller cuts, and blood mixed with rain dripped freely.

"Get up," I growled.

The driver didn't make the right move. Instead, he curled up into a tight ball and closed his eyes. There is nothing in God's worlds that I detest more than a spineless coward; to be brave when you feel safe to attack the weak, and then whimper and flee like a chicken when the fight comes to you. I never imagined that I could feel so much contempt for something so little. Not even Lucifer, with all his lying, trickery and conniving ways had made me loathe him to this extent. This was a weasel, a coward, a worm. The fire engulfing my hands intensified as I bent down and grabbed the driver by the lapels of his coat and yanked him to his feet. He screeched in pain as my fiery hands scorched the sides of his neck.

"Your soul may be safe for now, but I'll be back sooner than you think," I hissed, and backhanded him across the face, branding him with the mark of the serpent.

TWENTY-EIGHT

The light in me was dead, and all I felt was outrage. A far more oppressive darkness had engulfed my soul and brought out in me the angst of anger, fear and sadness. *Hulk angry, Hulk smash* was a joke compared to what I wanted to do. His anger was momentary. Mine was eternal and unrelenting.

I dropped the driver and shot into the air. A part of me wanted the hunt, the chase for the killer, to engage in a game where the outcome was obvious to me but yet unsettled for him. I wanted Kay's killer to live in fear, to know that he was the hunted and I the hunter. To allow him a brief escape, a light where he would find hope like Kay had, and then hound him mercilessly until he begged me for death. But another part of me simply wanted the catch, the immediate sentencing and execution of a worthless existence, and that's what I went for. My redemption to Kay.

From my vantage point, I saw the killer's sedan race in my direction and knew he felt exhilarated thinking that he had escaped. He believed that I mistook the driver for him; how foolishly stupid. His thought, his last thought, *better him than me.* I'm sorry Jesus, but Man still hasn't learned that to find life he has to lose it, sacrifice it. And this one would wish that he had done unto others as he wished done to him.

It was time to quench hope, to rip it out from every possible crevasse of the killer's being. With the car only a few hundred feet from me, I allowed myself to fall through the sky like a massive meteor – a streak of hot blue, and landed in the street with a loud explosion. Chunks of concrete flew everywhere, denting cars, crashing into buildings, and smashing windows. It was a pre-apocalyptic moment and I enjoyed the Hulkish theatrics of it all, especially when I saw the look on the killer's face. I was on my knee like a football player waiting for the punt, the ball being the car that was shooting towards me. I smiled at the killer and he, in return, tried to do the only thing that he could; run me down. It was the perfect ending, the fight between metal and flesh. I heard the beast's engine wail as it lurched forward, succumbing to its commander's final order, and deliberately got to my feet. As the eternal harvester of souls I would forgo my existence to become the harvester of *one* life – the spoils of my war. And for that, I needed a majestic moment. I pushed back my wet hair and opened my arms wide in a great embrace. My wings, seldom used in the new world, snapped open behind me in a semicircle, their appearance even to me, magnificent; a pattern of inky-black feathers with tips of silver. I stood there squinting, momentarily silent and motionless, my eyes serpent-like in their narrow slits. Not that I needed a specific moment of advantage for my attack. What I wanted was to see the white of the killer's eyes, and I did. With our eyes locked, I forcefully brought my hands together in an ear splitting clap that sent out a thunderous shockwave in the direction of the speeding sedan. Cars flew to the sides and crashed into poles and walls while trees were ripped from their roots. Windows in the buildings on either side of the street exploded one after the other as the wave rippled its way to the killer, clearing the path for our final encounter. I didn't want anything in our way.

"You freak of nature!" were the only words the killer could muster before our worlds collided.

The impact was brutal but quite unlike what the killer expected. Metal bent, twisted and screeched as the sedan tore apart around me, its momentum relentlessly pushing it forward. I didn't flinch or move a muscle, but kept my eyes on my prize while the car ripped in half. But this wasn't the ending that I wanted for the killer. It wouldn't be that easy, generous or forgiving. I wanted him to suffer, to feel the agony and pain of loss. As soon as he was within my reach, I grabbed him and pulled him into my chest, my wings surrounding him in a protective cocoon. The protection, however, was momentary and from immediate physical damage. I wanted him to feel the agony I bore inside, what I had endured for him and his brethren throughout existence and how Man, *he*, had repaid that sacrifice. To bear one's own burden in silence is to accept loneliness, but to do it for mankind?

I opened the gateway to my soul and let everything loose, knowing well that his soul could not take it. The killer's eyes opened wide in horror as scenes from thousands of years of human carnage and atrocity flashed by in a violent slideshow. However, it wasn't the pain of war and destruction that drained the life from his body and made his heart wither like a prune. It was the towering feeling of loss, desolation and hopelessness that pulled at his being and finally swallowed him. But he only fell into complete darkness, the death of light and hope, when he saw the life-movie of the girl he had shot dead. My Kay. My little one.

"No, no, no! I had no choice..." his mind shrieked in silence. "What can I do to be saved?"

I looked down at his contorted face. Black veins had webbed their way from his temples and forehead to his eyes, ears, and cheeks all the way down to his neck. His skin was leathery-old and decrepit, and his eyes filmy and no longer vivid with the spark of life. Tears rolled down his cheeks in a continuous and uncontrollable stream. Dr. Who would be proud of *my* weeping angel.

"Nothing." That offer was not on the table.

I once argued with Michael about justice and punishment. The dangers of wanting to always see the good in Man and forgiving him in the hope of change. But what about the incorrigible ones? How could we justify their existence to the ones they wronged and the ones that they would wrong? No! All we accomplish by sparing the guilty is to threaten the innocent and plant the seed of chaos. Not anymore.

The night sky was angry and the storm clouds swirled and collided, unceremoniously unleashing Father's expression of violent displeasure. There was, however, nothing that He could do that was worse than what I had already committed myself to. I grinned, and with the killer still held hostage in his winged cage, leaped to the edge of the tallest building on the street. For a moment, I stood there and took in the miles and miles of city that spread out before me. To me, it was an inferno of lost souls, but soon they would no longer be my problem. I looked over my shoulder, and for an instant, was disappointed not to see Michael. I guess some part of me wanted him to be there, to challenge me so that I could justify myself. I turned, opened my wings and released the killer to the night air, but before he fell, grabbed him by the collar and held him over the ledge like a kitten in a cat's mouth. He was limp and swung from side to side with the growing wind. I thought that I had overdone it. That he wouldn't even be aware of his death, but cockroaches don't die that easily, and he opened his red, bulging eyes and looked at me. I took Kay's necklace from my pocket and swung it in front of him like a pendulum before slipping it around his neck. At that instant, Bran landed on my shoulder and pecked me gently on the neck. He was telling me that he had my back and giving me the good-to-go.

"Please… please… I'm sorry… I had no choice…"

As if having or not having a choice meant anything to me. Who you are is not defined by what you believe or what you say. Ultimately, it's the legacy you leave behind defined by what you've done and the choices that you've made *because* of your circumstances. So, yes, he did have a choice and so did I. "As promised, tonight you die," I hissed.

I guess it was at that moment that Father fully realized that I was not going to stop. That Lucifer would finally have me and become my lord and keeper. For a split-second, the sky became darker than black, a complete void, and there was no angel made of gold to stop me. My ground shook as Lucifer reveled below in his palace of fire and stone, and then my world was mercilessly assaulted by lighting after lightning as I slowly opened my grip and let the killer drop.

"Father, we can try and try, but in the end our souls cry for what we truly are, and I can't change who I am. Please forgive me even though I know what I've done."

TWENTY-NINE

The hooded figure was impassive. No comment, no sigh, no goddamn anything. Maybe she was just like me, hard and careless, and counseling wasn't part of her job description. Or maybe I wasn't a good story teller, and what I hoped would move her to understand why I did what I did wasn't reason enough. Or, it was simply because she was a woman; harder, harsher and more determined. Either way, it didn't matter because now we were in it together, and she would be the one to have to deliver me to my fate.

"It's time. He'll be here soon." I paused, but the trend continued and there was no sign of any interest to find out who. No concern, no desire, no curiosity. Maybe she was a statue, but interestingly enough, now her absolute disinterest made me smile. She was simply better suited than me for this job, and I admired that – more broken and callous from the get-go. This, unlike me, gave her a chance to survive because in the beginning I did care; and ultimately at my core I never stopped caring. I stood up and hesitated, then picked up the leaf with my initial on it and put it in the pocket of my overcoat. I couldn't quite see, but knew that the hooded figure was intently watching my every move. Her focus was the leaf, her first and possibly most significant assignment. She probably wanted to keep it as a memento; maybe I would give it to her later if she said *pretty please.* But then, surprisingly she did something quite uncharacteristic by looking up at me. It was a fleeting moment, and in that instant I thought I saw the shimmer of what looked like tears, but then she stood and her face was once again lost in the blackness of the room.

I walked around the table in silence, heading for the hall she had come from. As I reached her, I smelled the distant fragrance of jasmine and roses. It was a jolt to my system. I froze, but before I could say anything she turned and walked away. I followed her, my heart and mind ablaze. Was this a punishment for my actions? Was she to bear my cross because of my defiance? Had I defined and sealed her fate? As these thoughts bludgeoned me, we entered the Room of Candles.

The room, with its innumerous rows of living candles, was eerily dark, and shadows swayed and danced everywhere. I stopped in the middle of the room and watched the hooded figure make her way to the far wall where my scythe was resting in the shadows. I guess the moment had come for me to truly step down by passing on the one thing that I had made but which ultimately defined me. I waited and watched, expecting her to simply take it, but she didn't. She stood there with her back to me, her arms weighing beside her and her head bowed in what seemed to be more shame than respect.

"Look at me! Talk to me!"

I took a step towards her, but before I could go any further a subtle breeze wafted across the room. The candles flickered briefly, and the dim yellowish light turned a dark orange. For the moment, I had to let it go – let her go – and switch gears. The man of the hour had arrived.

"You couldn't have done that. You shouldn't have done that. You manipulated her into that alley."

A shadow jumped out from the corner closest to the hooded figure and with it Lucifer in his human form. He glanced over, acknowledging her presence, then walked past her and planted himself between us. The hooded figure didn't move or react.

"Dear brother, *I* didn't do any such thing. Kay's death is the result of the tragedy, or better, the travesty that is Man. You know it, and I know it. Or else, we wouldn't be standing here now." Lucifer rubbed his goatee and looked at me with those pale eyes. "Now, I believe who couldn't or shouldn't have done what they did is *you*. But between us, didn't you enjoy the freedom? The power to impart justice the way *you* wanted – the way it was meant to be as Azrail?

"Yes." There was no point denying it. "And now, I will pay the price for that freedom."

"Good." Lucifer made a sharp motion with his hand. "Come and kneel before your master."

For a moment, contempt overwhelmed me, and I wanted nothing more than to engage in a self-destructing battle that would end it all. But there was no fight left in me and that momentary rush was replaced by a sense of resignation. I walked to Lucifer, each step heavier and more demanding than any fight or challenge, but to sacrifice was to love. I stopped and bowed in feigned respect.

"As fearful as a master can possibly be, I will always be a more dangerous servant." I surreptitiously looked up at the hooded figure and hoped that she would one day understand. Unlike me, her desire to be kind was far greater than her need to always be righteous, and a patient heart that listens has the power to transform. She would do a better job than me and maybe even save Man. "To your enemies, of course."

"I'll keep that in mind as I break you to mold you. Now, *kneel!*" Lucifer grabbed my shoulder with one hand and forced me down. My lack of resistance surprised him, and he grinned as I dropped to my knees. "You've been such a pain in my side for so long, brother, but I wanted the rose and I was never afraid of a few thorns."

I didn't look at him, but kept my head down. Suddenly, he grasped my hair and violently yanked my head back, forcing me to look up into his face. I felt the bones in my back crack as my neck snapped upward. The muscles and tendons holding my head screamed in pain as fire shot up and down my spine, but my mouth did not utter the slightest sound nor my face reveal the least discomfort. It was hard to contain, but I wouldn't give him the satisfaction. Lucifer, with his eyes riveted on mine, bent down until his face was only an inch away. I could feel the warmth of his breath on my face, and it didn't smell putrid as I imagined it would. It had a hint of apple.

"You're very fluent in silence when talking isn't wise. Continue like this and we shall *all* get along just fine." He looked back at the hooded figure without moving his head. The message was clear. "I once vowed that I would have your soul, and by *ME*, that day has come!"

He could have it, I was done with it. I had run it high and low well past its expiration date, and there was nothing that he could do to me that I feared. I was ready to succumb to anything as long as she was left out of it, but then as if answering my thoughts, Lucifer released my head and turned. He stood there in silence behind the hooded figure. My muscles tensed, and I was ready to lunge, to defend her, when I realized that he wasn't really looking at her, but past her towards the wall. His focus was my scythe. Bran was also there, perched on its handle, and I wondered when he arrived. He looked venomous, and his beady eyes were riveted on Lucifer. I knew he wanted to peck his eyes out, but he was obeying me by staying clear. Lucifer stretched out his arm and summoned the scythe, but like a beast that was being forced into captivity, it shook violently and resisted. Bran cawed in anger and jumped off. He looked at me for approval, one last attack to permanently mark the day, but I shook my head. I didn't want him in Lucifer's way. He was to guide and protect the hooded figure after I was gone. Lucifer tried again, this time with his whip, only to be denied by an even more explosive rejection as the two made contact and blue and red lightning flew in every direction. Bran did what I wanted to do. He voiced his pleasure at Lucifer's rejection by circling the space above the scythe and cawing repeatedly. I managed a smirk, but made him stop and quiet down. I was going to be the only target today.

Lucifer slowly turned to me. "Apparently, I'm not the only one to remember or hold a grudge. There is common blood between it and me." His voice was calm, almost amused by the scythe's behavior. He walked past me and I looked down to hide my satisfaction. "There's no rush, it *will* yield and learn to obey me," he said, and stood behind me. "But the one thing that will not, and it's quite apparent that he is a chip off of the old block, is that annoying bird."

I couldn't see Lucifer, but my head zinged with dread. Lucifer never made empty threats and as I turned to Bran, I saw his eyes glow red and he tried to caw. My companion, the one friend that accompanied me throughout the centuries and sat by me on those long and destructive nights, dropped to the floor dead. I looked at him one last time and mourned. Soon, I would be laying with him.

"Now, back to business!"

Having Lucifer stand behind me was the ultimate threat, but to be willingly at his mercy was a far greater challenge than anything I had ever faced. I once told a great leader that you never turn your back on danger and try to run away because that would only heighten the threat. Instead you cut it in half by meeting it promptly and ferociously. He did and he won. But here I was on my knees with my back to the true definition of danger, and my will for defiance was overpowered by the necessity for sacrifice. I did not feel elated, but I also didn't look at it as humiliation.

I looked up and noticed that the hooded figure had turned and was facing me. Her face continued obscured by her hood, and she was once again absentmindedly caressing the pendant around her neck. Then, slowly, purposefully she lowered her hand and revealed it to me. My heart skipped a beat as the nine-pointed-star shone momentarily before disappearing within the folds of her cloak. It *was* her, my little one. Before I could say or do anything, I heard a swishing sound behind me and the hooded figure gasped. I twisted my head to the side just in time to see a black talon flash across my vision with Lucifer in his beastly form. I felt no tug or resistance as it cut through my leather overcoat and slashed open the skin from my left shoulder blade to the middle of my back. Pain seared through me as I gritted my teeth in an attempt to smother the reflex to cry out. Before I could recompose, however, I felt the steel-like edge of the talon once again against my skin, cutting my back open this time from the right shoulder blade down and across. I lost control, and even with my teeth clenched together and my jaw locked shut, I heard myself grunt in pain. A much louder and anguished scream, however, overwhelmed the room.

"No…" It was the hooded figure.

"Don't worry, my angel, I'm just marking the X for my treasure. The best is yet to come."

Lucifer's words were a jumble. The pain was so intense that I felt myself passing out, but her outcry filled me with new determination and I held on. My back was cut to shreds and my muscles burned as blood streamed to the floor, but I used every ounce of my will to keep my wings from folding out. If he wanted them, he would have to pry them out himself. X marks the spot, but unlike popular belief, it's not where the treasure is buried and yes, where the executioner aims and delivers the final blow to condemned prisoners. Lucifer wanted my wings; my prized treasure was his bull's-eye.

Even though I was prepared for the assault, I never sensed it come, and the jolt from the impact took my breath. Lucifer rammed something cold and hard into the open wound and was using it as a lever to force my wings out. Every nerve shrieked and fired in agony, but I remained silent. Cold sweat covered my forehead and dripped from my brow into my eyes and down my face. Finally, as my body weakened and my being was nothing but raw pain, I succumbed and my wings opened to the world with a majestic swish. I was so weak and dizzy that the motion made me fall forward, and I had to use my hands and arms to keep me from crashing to the floor. From my half prostrated position, I looked up at the hooded figure, and this time I was sure that the reflection that I saw was her tears. Why was she still here? She had delivered me and that in itself was more than she had to do. For me, to have her witness giving myself without resistance, looked humiliating. I was afraid she wouldn't understand. I still wanted to be her hero; her angel.

Lucifer roared with delight and lowered himself onto one knee beside me. He brought his head down and cocked it sideways so that his eyes were level with mine, obstructing my view. There was an unusual glint, a dancing fire, in his eyes as he smiled, and for the first time I saw what it looked like when the devil was happy; a black hole where existence has no past or future.

"I waited a very long time for this. There were times when I could have hurt you, taught you a good lesson, but it wouldn't be memorable enough – as you yourself once said. So, I waited and waited until you acted like Man and gave me the perfect opening. When you started caring, you became vulnerable, but when you fell in love you became a wise fool who disregarded himself. Not that I didn't weave the path you walked, but the choices were all yours." Lucifer grabbed my throat, his talons sinking into my neck, and pushed me back so I could once more see the hooded figure staring at us. "Take a good look. Man never controls his own fate. It's the women in his life that do it for him." He let go and stood. "Remember this?" he said, and drew something out from behind him and held it in front of me. It was a bloody scimitar, the one he had used as a lever.

I immediately recognized the ornate handle of the scimitar. It was Benaiah's sword, King Solomon's executioner. The last time I saw it was on the day when Solomon had to decide the fate of a baby. Because the truth was elusive, he asked Benaiah to cut the child in half and give each women their fair share, and by doing so revealed the truth and proved his wisdom. It was time for me to do the same.

"It used to be an eye for an eye and a tooth for a tooth, but I'm going to change that a little *and* add compounded interest. Let's see, how about two wings for my broken horn?" Lucifer planted his feet squarely on the ground and raised the weapon above his head. "That was rhetorical, of course."

I looked over my shoulder at my wings and for an instant felt nostalgic. They were awe inspiring, but as a fallen angel they would never grow back. I turned my head to the ground and nodded my consent. I heard the familiar sound of steel cutting through air and gritted my teeth ready for impact. Suddenly, there was thunder and a flash of blinding light as the door to the room exploded, sending shards of metal and wood everywhere. I heard Lucifer roar in frustration as he stumbled backwards. The scimitar missed its mark, crashing on the stone floor beside my leg. The hooded figure was thrown back hard against the wall where my scythe was resting and fell to the floor unconscious. I looked up and there, standing in the doorframe, was Michael.

"Azrail, no! It's Kay, she's…"

I raised my left arm and fired. The blue fireball hit Michael square in the chest and propelled him backwards. He smashed against the wall of the hall behind him and fell. He and his armor now had some memorable dents and bruises.

"This is between Lucifer and me, so stay out of it. What's done is done!" I was furious. He didn't know anything about Kay, but wanted to tell me what to do. I couldn't let Lucifer find out, just yet, who the hooded figure was, and it was up to me to protect her. To do that, I had to do this all the way. "Just make sure you protect the new angel." With that, I fired three more fireballs at the ceiling above the door.

Michael, half crouched and on his side, reached into his pocket. "Azrail, you don't understand…" The explosions drowned his words. The structure of the room shook violently as cracks spider-webbed their way up the walls, and then with a mighty crash, the ceiling started to cave in. I saw Michael jerk his hand free from his pocket and throw something shiny through the door right before the rest of the ceiling collapsed, cutting us from the world and further interruptions. I tried to see what the little object was, but it bounced across the floor and disappeared in the rubble. It didn't really matter anyway. I didn't care.

Still on my hands and knees, I turned to the hooded figure lying on the ground unconscious and clambered my way towards her. For the first time that day, I could see her partially uncovered face, and it hurt more than any physical damage that Lucifer had inflicted on me. Before I reached her, however, Lucifer's foot crashed down on my lower back and pinned me to the ground.

"Don't worry about her, she'll get used to my parties; maybe. This isn't Georgia and Johnny isn't invited. A fiddle made of gold isn't much of a prize when you can't hold it long enough to play; it's just too damn heavy. I prefer mine, because in the end I always get what I go up to get. I *love* Man, they've got so much of me." Lucifer laughed heartily. "When I play, everyone has to dance, baby."

Lucifer took his foot off of my back but immediately grabbed the neckline of my coat, his claws ripping into the back of my neck, and yanked me back into a kneeling position.

"Let's finish what we started, shall we?" He took a step forward and stood behind me to my right. "Again, rhetorical in case you were wondering." As he raised the scimitar, the hooded figure moaned softly. I looked up at her, only a foot away, and our eyes met as Lucifer lustily swung the sword down in a precise arc, slashing my right wing off with a clean cut at its base. My wing, with its black feathers adorned in silver, fell to the floor with a soft thud, but unlike repentance offered to the owner of a branded leaf, it was part of my penance. It confirmed my fall and toned my menial future.

The hooded figure's horrified shriek filled the room. I, in turn, choked and my scream was caught inside me, but not in pain. My mind and eyes were at war as I looked into the face that I knew so well and yet did not know.

"Who are you?" Somewhere in my past I knew her. Her resemblance to Kay. And then I remembered. "Martha?" The name came out as a whisper and was almost lost in the pounding coming from behind the fallen walls as Michael tried to breach the room.

"I'm so sorry… I didn't know!" cried the girl. A torrent of tears poured from her eyes, and I knew that she was crying, not for herself, but for me.

Lucifer stepped over my legs and positioned himself for the next blow. "How touching. If you were a saint, girl, all of humanity would be cured. Now, hold your tears a bit longer because I'm not done!"

Before Lucifer could swing, Martha got to her knees and threw herself in-between us. "Please, you got what you wanted. He's here now. Use him, but let him be."

"What? And have a lopsided trophy? No, I can't do that, especially because I was thinking of putting his wings behind my *throne made of stone*." He said the last three words in a mocking rhyme and smiled. "I almost feel like dancing. I think I'm getting giddy with joy." Then, instantly, his face once again turned cold and beastly. "But I'm not happy. I *want* my other wing," he sneered.

To me, nothing that was going on behind me made any sense. "Martha, why?" was the only thing I could say.

Lucifer roughly pushed her aside, and she fell to the ground beside me, but I kept my head bowed and did not look at her. I couldn't. Where was Kay? "Enough of this! How many times has the good guy, *me* of course, paused at the freaking finish line for some stupid reason and then lost the damn race because the so-called hero does something unbelievably spectacular and definitely impossible?" Lucifer lifted the scimitar above his head. "All the time in the movies, but in real life. *Never!*" Once again I heard the swishing sound of steel cutting through air and clenched my gut in reaction. I heard the thud, and then pain took hold and seared through me like hot lava. I fell to my side, and there was nowhere to look but at Martha.

My body convulsed uncontrollably, and soon I was lying in a pool of my own blood. If I were my old self, the cuts and my wings would heal. Now, I wasn't sure how I would recover, but I knew that Lucifer would not let me die. He wanted his high-born slave.

Martha crawled over and held my face. "I'm so sorry..." she sobbed. "I did it for Kay."

"How touching. Do what you want to get what you want and in the process indiscriminately destroy others – in this case my dear brother. Don't get me wrong, I truly appreciate that, but then to sob like a child and say you're *so sorry*. Hmm..." Lucifer stopped and scratched his head in feigned wonder. "I've seen it work over and over and it never ceases to surprise the *me* out of me, but my bet is on a different kind of ending here. Man is more forgiving than an angel, so go ahead, reminisce and catch up. I'll just stand here in the corner and enjoy my show."

I felt drops on my face and realized that my eyes were closed. I opened them and was again shocked to see the eyes that should have been Kay's looking down at me with so much regret. "What happened?" My voice sounded alien even to me. My breath came in spurts and I was lightheaded, causing the burning sensation in my back to feel less intense.

"My life ended the day that man dragged me out of my car but left my baby to die." Martha grabbed my hand and brought it to her chest. Then, slowly, she wrapped the fingers of her left hand around my index finger. My heart stopped and I was suddenly alert. "You were there, and I knew what you were. I begged you and begged you to save her, to take me instead. But you just sat there by her and looked at me without showing the least bit of compassion or understanding. I hated you so much." She was sobbing again. "How could you sit there and let her innocently play with your fingers when you knew she was about to die?"

I looked at her, but there was no answer. I had nothing to say. She wouldn't understand.

Martha stifled a sob and continued. "I wrestled with them and pleaded for someone to save my baby, but no one moved. It was horrific. People just stood watching as my car kept sinking, but I was *not* going to let that piece of metal become my baby's coffin. That's when *he* approached me." For the first time since we met that day, the hooded figure avoided my eyes and looked away. "It was simple enough, my afterlife for my baby's mortal life," she said in a whisper and turned to look at me again. "I became Faust."

"No! No! No!" I gritted my teeth in frustration. "The young boy who gave his life for Mary did it on his own. It was his choice, his free will. That split-second decision came from his heart and was his alone." I pointed at Lucifer. "He feeds Man's greed with promises of material anything – life, fame, and money and that boy relinquished it all." I looked down at Martha's delicate fingers. It was my fault. "He tricked you."

Martha shook her head and smiled, but her eyes betrayed her sadness. "I know. Mary got sick and we battled that sickness all of her life. We were cheated; Mary, from a life fully lived and I…"

"Hey, hey, hey… I never promised a full and happy life," interrupted Lucifer, and grinned. "You should always read the fine print." He looked at Martha and motioned for her to continue. "Please, don't stop. This is an Oscar winning performance. If I *had* a heart, it would be bleeding with sorrow!"

I looked at Lucifer and if there was any piece of Man in me, it would strike a deal with him and then smack the grin off his face and break every bone in his body. But alas, I wasn't Man and in no condition to fight, but seeing Martha unperturbed helped calm me a bit. Grief works like a shield since nothing can penetrate the black hole that it leaves in your heart.

"But there was Kay to warm my heart and remind me that my sacrifice was worth it," Martha continued, as if there had been no interruption. "If I hadn't done what I did, she would never have existed and that alone justified everything." The mention of Kay's name made my heart skip a beat. Martha noticed the tension in my body and pressed my hand. "I'm sure you agree."

I nodded. If only the world had more Kays.

"That day on the street, when you came to take Mary for a second time, was one of the hardest of my life. There had not been a day that I didn't hate you and blame you for what I was forced to do. But it also, in a twisted way, offered me relief because I somehow fooled myself into believing that it would all end then and there and free me," said Martha, and added with emphasis while motioning to Lucifer, "*of him.*"

She took a deep breath, again choking back her tears, and in that moment I became aware of my body. My blood felt feverish and cold at the same time as it rushed through me. It was a sensation that I had felt many times when I was hurt and recovering, but never to this extent. Before I could do a mental check, however, Martha continued and my attention was once more fully on her.

"Mary asked me to leave and I knew that it was time. It broke my heart, but she wanted to be with you alone, and although I couldn't imagine why, I acquiesced because I trusted her judgment. How can you ever say no to the wish of a dying child?" She looked at me and this time the smile, ever so filled with lamentation, was real. "I'm glad I did because Kay needed you; needed you to protect her. But you also needed her to remind you of your humanity. Through her, I finally got to see through you and forgive you."

Martha bent down and kissed my forehead. "You were Kay's angel in every way, and as time passed, I started to believe that the nightmare was over. I ignored that dreaded feeling of Lucifer always lurking in the shadows and since he didn't show up personally, I didn't go looking. I naively believed that he had no hold over me now that Mary was gone. But then he came, as I always feared he would, and made me the Lazarus of hell. To collect his debt, he resurrected me after you delivered my soul, and all I had to do was play a role, be the mistress of death to the angel of death. I loved you, but I loved Kay more. There was never any doubt in him that I would do anything to save her."

"Save her?" I said in a rage. "You condemned her by not telling me when you had the chance. I was the only one who could have saved her from him!" I forgot myself and tried to get up, only to fall back in pain.

"Brother, brother... these souls are not there for your saving. They will always do in the end, what they want to and Kay was no exception. But I never had a chance with her as you should well remember." Lucifer chuckled and from within the rubble picked up the shiny object that Michael had thrown. "I can see how you would imagine saving her from that vile man and the grip of death, but what Michael was trying to tell you was that…" he stopped and held the nine-pointed-star up for me to see, his eyes in complete rapture, "*Kay* is alive!" With that, he tossed the pendant and it landed just short of my reach. "You should learn to listen, not that it would make any difference now."

I wasn't sure if I had heard right. How could that be? I saw Kay die. No, I actually watched her die through her memory. And the one thing that no being can tamper with is the memories of the soul. I looked from Lucifer's smug face to Martha and back, and I could tell that what he said was true. The unnatural exultation that exuded from him was proof.

"That's how I saved her," whispered Martha.

"I don't understand. I was in her memory… I *felt* her die." My eyes quickly snapped to and from the pendant lying on the ground just beyond my reach. "I took that from Kay's slain body. I wanted to make her killer feel her life as he fell to his death. But now…" My voice trailed off. I felt a strange fluttering in my chest.

"He came to me," Martha started, motioning to Lucifer, "and said that it was finally time for payback. I didn't know what he wanted from me, but it didn't matter because I wasn't going to do it. Mary died years ago and with you delivering my soul I felt free for the first time in almost fifty years. So I refused. But then, he gave me this," Martha touched the nine-pointed-star hanging from her neck, "and showed me Kay's memory of that day years ago at school. I was terrified to find out that he had the courage to approach her even with you protecting her. But what shocked me even more was Kay willingly giving him Mary's necklace to save someone she didn't even know. And then, he showed me *his* memory and how you recovered the necklace for Kay – or at least what you believed was her necklace, and that's when I knew that even with your protection she would never be safe. He was too devious and twisted; and she was too kind and altruistic. He would use that against her and make her give him her soul."

"I don't understand!" I glared at Martha, but my frustration and anger stemmed from my own failure. "What other necklace?" Even as the words left my mouth, I knew the answer but didn't want to acknowledge the simple truth; Lucifer had maneuvered me to kill.

"Yessss," hissed Lucifer, "that is the question. *I* had a cunning plan!" He roared with laughter as a black adder appeared over his shoulder and snaked its way around his left arm. "Do continue, child. *Tell* him."

"He tricked you, and he would trick her for her soul. It was as simple as that. I knew that I was trapped, but I wasn't helpless. He wanted you, not Kay, and because I knew that there was a deal to be made, I made it." Martha paused and lowered her gaze, and I saw a tear drop to her lap. "You were Kay's angel. You would have done the same to save her." She looked up and her eyes found mine again. "No?"

It was true, I would do anything to protect Kay, but I was still mad at Martha for not having confided in me. In a calm voice, or at least as calm as possible for me, I said, "Tell me what you did. What did he want from you?" My mind was already racing ahead. I wanted to find a way to see Kay, make sure that she really was alive before it was all over.

"He took me to a dark street and showed me two men lurking in the shadows. It didn't make much sense, but when I saw Kay enter the alley I knew that I would do anything that he asked for; he also knew that. And I didn't care that he was manipulating me. If this, somehow, was Kay's fate I was the only one who could change it. So, we made a deal. I would help him trick you and in return he would save Kay and never approach her again. All I had to do was take a leaf to a place he couldn't go and then die in Kay's place."

Lucifer had planned everything to the last detail. He knew that I would know he had been in the room, so he sent a simple soul with no footprint to do his dirty work and plant the leaf with Kay's name on it. "What do you mean die in Kay's place? It was her that I felt, it *was* Kay." I put my hand in my pocket and felt the soft, suede-like texture of the leaf.

"Yes and no." Martha, for the second time, gently touched my face. "The pendant you took back that night from him was a copy. He had planned it all along knowing you would go and get it back. From that night on, all of Kay's memories were stored on that pendant. That's what you saw when you touched it."

I took out the leaf and looked at the letter *M*. Soon, it would be time to let the leaf run its course.

"When I returned, after planting the leaf, I saw Kay running down the alley and for a moment thought that she would get away; that I made the deal for nothing. But for his plan to work, Kay *had* to die. That's when one of the men got up and shot me." Martha stopped and wiped the tears from her eyes.

I looked at her and felt sad. For the second time, she had given up her soul to Lucifer to save others. She deserved more than becoming his mistress, but never had a chance. She was caught in the crossfire of my war with Lucifer; the war that I lost. I reached up with the leaf still in my hand and grabbed her teary-hand. As our fingers embraced, the leaf quivered slightly and we saw it glow as it completed its purpose. Neither of us, however, let go.

"He kept his word and saved Kay. I don't know how that happened, but I was one with her for that instant, the moment that the bullet hit. And then you were there looking down at me, at us. I wanted to somehow let you know, but the next thing I remember is standing outside the room where you were waiting. He was ecstatic, but still wanted more. That's when he gave me the original necklace to use as a message. But I felt ashamed and hid it until it was time for me to take you to him."

Suddenly, there was a jabbing pain in my chest. My body shook violently as flesh, bone and cartilage tore and snapped all the way to my back where my wings had been. I could barely breathe, the pressure in my ears and eyes so great that I wasn't sure I would survive. Slowly, I felt my body rise from the ground and float in midair as if suspended by my waist, my limbs and head pulled down like anchors. Martha let go of my hand and stood, but before she could do anything there was an explosion of blue light, and I fell back with a thump and rolled to my side exhausted. Martha was thrown back and was lying on her back on the ground by my butchered wings.

In my half-conscious state, I noticed Lucifer look at me, and I saw that old-time intensity in his eyes. But there was also something else, a sense of urgency that had not been there moments before. "Story time is over," he said, and walked to me. He was ready to deliver the final blow.

Whatever just happened to me drained my body of its last resources, leaving me completely helpless and my eyes hazy and unfocused. I leaned on my elbow and noticed the light reflect off of a metallic object close to my shoulder. I pushed myself to my knees, on all fours, and picked it up. It was the fake pendant and I was immediately sucked into its memory. I could see feet dangling in midair off of a building and then the concrete floor rushing up at me. The body I was witnessing crashed to the floor but did not break. And then Lucifer's raspy voice invaded my mind and broke the trance as I saw Michael's fading image stand up.

"That's the perfect position, no need to move."

I felt the cold, steel blade of the scimitar rest on the back of my neck. I guess I wasn't a worthy minion, or the fact that even as his slave I would make his existence a living hell wasn't very appealing to him. Either way, the end of our war was what it was.

"Before I send you on your way…" Lucifer paused. "Where is it that you *would* go? I'm not even sure. But there is a first time for everything. Anyway, I want to leave you with a lasting thought, impression, vision… something deeply disturbing and grotesque. An image that will stay with you, burned in your mind's eye forever." Lucifer chuckled and with his free hand motioned to the wall across the room. The surface of the wall rippled like a pool and slowly an image started to form. I was still having trouble with my eyes, but Martha's gasp confirmed what I feared. Lucifer's threat was personal to both of us.

"That's Kay in my home," Martha said in a barely audible voice. "What are you doing?" Martha slowly got to her feet, holding her left arm in pain.

Again, as if on cue, my heart skipped a beat at the mention of Kay's name, but before I could say anything Lucifer interrupted. "I'm not doing anything," was his silky response. "But that man at the corner of the street below, I'm not too sure about." The image on the wall zoomed out and shifted to the street outside Martha's apartment. There was a man standing at the corner. As my eyes finally cleared and I was able to focus, I recognized the branding on his face. How could I not? I gave it to him earlier that day; it was the driver of the sedan.

The sound that left my mouth was indistinguishable, but its intensity caused the candle lights to tremble and dance. I made a move to get up, but the steel blade on my neck kept me in check as it cut through my skin and kept me on fours. I felt the blood gush out and leave a warm trail on my skin as it rolled down around my neck and dripped to the floor. This was what he wanted, what he had planned for so long.

"Easy, brother, easy…" coaxed Lucifer.

"But you promised. We had a deal…" pleaded Martha and took a tentative step toward Lucifer.

Lucifer tilted his head to the side and looked at her amused. "And you believed me?" He pointed at Martha and continued, "You yourself said I'm the devil, so it only makes sense that you should know that when you're in bed with the devil, *you're in bed* with the devil. How can there be any confusion there? If my word meant anything, I'd still be an angel."

As much as I wanted to get up and rip my deceiving brother's tongue out of his mouth, Martha's penetrating stare was even more damaging. Actually, it said it all: *don't ever betray a woman.*

"Ah, woman, that's a pretty cold look. I'll be right with you after I take care of my dear brother. A trip to my humble abode will warm you right up." Lucifer took a step to my left and raised the scimitar. "This time, it will be his pretty, little head."

For the third time that night, I heard steel slice the air as it came down on me, and I was grateful for how sharp Lucifer kept his blades.

Instinctively, the muscles on my back and neck tightened as I braced for the impact that never came. Instead, there was the piercing shriek of a wounded animal. I looked up confused just as Lucifer's right forearm and scimitar fell past my head to the ground. The shock of what I witnessed and the image of Martha holding my bloody scythe stumped me for an instant. But any instant is too long when Lucifer in concerned; especially a wounded Lucifer. I knew there would be immediate retaliation and I lunged at his legs hoping that he would engage me and not Martha, but my body was too broken to react fast enough. Lucifer kicked out his right knee and caught me on the side of the head, sending me sprawling on the floor.

Martha lifted the scythe and brought it down in an arc aimed at Lucifer's neck. I was surprised at her dexterity and handling of my weapon, and if it had been directed at anyone or anything but Lucifer, the strike was fast and precise enough to end it all right then. But this was Lucifer and to cut him down you had to be God. Almost in slow motion, he lazily lifted his left arm and used his talons to deflect the attack. Then, with a cruel smile, he impaled Martha in the chest and lifted her off her feet. Martha gasped and dropped the scythe.

"No!" I jumped to my feet. Before I could do anything else, Lucifer threw Martha's body at me. I caught her and we both crashed to the floor. She was half on top of me with her back pressed to my chest. Her breath came in wheezing spurts and I felt the warmth of her blood as it soaked my shirt and ran down my stomach. Slowly, carefully, I slid out from under her, propped her against the wall, and got to my knees. I gently touched her cheek, and she slowly moved her head to the side and focused on me, her eyes already lost in the half-life of afterlife. There was nothing to say, but I saw that behind that curtain of sadness in her eyes there was a glimmer of relief. She was saved.

"That's the devil's kingdom minus one," she said in a low whisper and took my hand with difficulty. "Now go and save Kay and it will become minus two." Martha closed her eyes and with a slight but confident smile exhaled for the last time as her hand slid from mine and fell to the floor. I let my eyes slowly wash over her face, her resemblance to Kay uncanny, and prayed for her soul. The sorrow that engulfed me, however, was because of my impotence to save Kay. Martha did what she had to do to give Kay a chance to survive, and like she said, now it was my turn to do the same; to once again be her angel. But how?

I looked away from Martha and noticed her left hand still resting on her chest where she was wounded. At first, I didn't see it but then noticed her clenched fist holding on to the bloody leaf with my name. I had completely forgotten about it and could barely make out the letters *Ma*. How could this be? There had to be a way for me to save Kay before my end. With a tremulous hand I reached down and gently retrieved the leaf. It was crumpled, folded in a way that hid the rest of the letters. I paused, my fingers caressing the softness of its surface, and a part of me wanted to leave it that way; it was what it was. The angry part that for so long had become my identity, however, wanted to see more. It wanted to witness the sentencing of my soul, my name inscribed in gold for services rendered. Slowly, I slipped my thumb under the fold and pushed the leaf open, revealing the full name: *Martha*. I shut my eyes in shock. Instantly, Michael's image filled my mind.

Lucifer was sitting prostrated on the floor with his severed forearm aligned perfectly with the rest of his arm. Suddenly, fire flew from his fingertips – both left and right hands, and like a snake he hissed with delight as his tongue slithered from side to side extinguishing the flames except for his left index finger. Then, he slowly pointed the flame at his wounded arm and cauterized it back where it belonged.

"You shouldn't have done that," I growled. "She didn't deserve to die like that." I stood, and Lucifer did the same. We were standing face to face, both aware of what was coming next.

"Brother, brother. There are no actions in this world that do not bring about consequences, and the punishment dished out in this particular case certainly fit the crime." Lucifer held up his right arm and flexed his fingers while scrutinizing his forearm. "In a relationship, scars are inevitable."

I nodded and felt the scars on my back. "You gave me a couple of good ones yourself. I hope you were careful to make them symmetrical. Like you said, I don't want my new look to be lopsided." With that, I took off my tattered and blood soaked coat and shirt and threw them on the ground. Behind Lucifer, I saw Kay's reflected image get up from the couch in Martha's apartment. She was getting ready to leave. "You were wrong about Michael. What he wanted to say was that I didn't kill anyone after all. As usual, my dear brother butted in and saved that wretched lowlife. I guess I owe him big time."

The *swoosh* and pop of my new wings opening was exhilarating. It was like being infused with new blood, a kind of wild and uncontained energy that surges through predators when they are on the hunt. My body suddenly felt electric. But the best prize was seeing the momentary shock on Lucifer's face. "No more Mr. Nice Guy. From now on, we're playing on hard-mode with default weapons and no bonuses!"

Lucifer was immediately back to his usual smug self, his countenance one of casual reflection. "I have to admit that I didn't see this coming," he said, and leered at me. "But do you really believe that with me in your way you will have time to save *her*?" Without turning, he motioned to the wall behind him. Kay was putting on her coat. "You always underestimate me, little brother. I'm too *me* not to have backup plans."

Surreptitiously, I glanced to the side, but there was no way that I could leave without fighting him. When I collapsed the ceiling to keep Michael out, I made the room impenetrable, and to break through I needed that freaking beast out of my way. I knew that this fight wasn't going to be a gentleman's duel; there was no honor here and certainly no judge or jury. It was going to be as dirty as it gets. Without warning, as my stare found his again, I extended my right arm and summoned my scythe. In response, he bared his teeth, and I saw his eyes twinkle and knew that I was a fraction too late. As my scythe flew through the air and into my open hand, I reflected on how much I hated the sound of cutting steel coming at me. I crouched, my body leaning to the side in defense, and held my arm up at an angle that positioned my scythe lengthwise over my head and shoulder in the path of the descending scimitar. My move was good, but not good enough. The scimitar deflected off of the handle of the scythe but continued its downward motion, barely missing my shoulder and slicing off the corner of my left wing. I screamed in frustration and pain, retracted my wings and rolled over my left shoulder in an attempt to put some distance between us and escape what I knew was coming next. In the background, I heard muffled explosions as Michael relentlessly tried to break into the room and wished that I could somehow tell him to stop and go to Kay; to save Kay.

The battle that followed was nothing short of barbaric, and I used every ounce of my newly found vigor to fend off his attack. Lucifer leaped the distance separating us and even before his feet crashed on the floor beside me, brought down the scimitar straight at my chest with all the power and weight of his body. With one knee on the ground, I pivoted backwards and held the scythe's shaft with both hands across my face as a shield. The collision of steel on steel was thunderous and the force almost broke my thumbs as I held fast. Before I could counter, however, Lucifer delivered another blow and another, sending sparks flying in every direction. I was being crushed, my knee breaking the wood floor and digging into the earth below as the onslaught continued. But somehow, even though I wasn't able to attack, I managed to parry every blow as I waited for a possible opening.

Lucifer wasn't concerned with my defense. To me it seemed like he wanted to slowly burry me into the ground as he relentlessly delivered stroke after stroke. Sweat rolled down my face and neck, and my arms and back screamed for reprieve. I was glad that Lucifer wasn't changing his pattern as I held on, but then I realized what he was doing. There were chips and gauges in the shaft of my scythe where he was concentrating his attack and soon it would break. I wondered what would give in first, the shaft or my arms. The answer came with the next blow as Lucifer smashed his scimitar once again on the shaft, but instead of lifting it and hitting again, he used it as a lever and pushed down with his body. I grunted in exhaustion and used everything I had to hold him back. My arm muscles burned and shook violently with the effort. He leaned closer and grabbed my neck with his free hand, his weight now fully on my arms. I could feel the heat from his body and smell the sweat as he exposed his fangs and gave a low, guttural growl. Slowly, my arms bent back and our faces came within inches of each other. This time, his breath was disgustingly putrid. I imagined him stuffing his face with rotten deviled eggs and smirked.

"Finding this amusing?" he sneered.

"No, not really," I grunted. "Just wondering if you had a mint." My back and legs were in distress and I knew that I would collapse at any second.

Lucifer relieved the pressure slightly. "You were always my favorite, little brother, but I see your despair for her and that tells me you care, that you still believe in these puny creatures of clay." He stopped and took a deep breath. When he started again, there was almost a hint of remorse in his words. "All these years, I thought that by showing you, you would finally understand. And even though I knew that you would never come to me willingly, I imagined that you would at least stay out of my way and allow me to do what had to be done. Now I know that will never be, and I have to finish what I started."

I couldn't hold on anymore, and before Lucifer had a chance to move, I collapsed to my side bringing him down with me. Unwittingly, it was my best move. As the scimitar slid across the scythe its blade caught on one of the chipped edges and ricocheted up gashing him across his left arm. He leaned back and roared in anger. I looked up and saw Kay in her coat but still in the apartment and on the phone - thank God for unsolicited sales calls. The distraction, however, cost me dearly. Lucifer struck me in the side of the head with the butt of the scimitar and at the same time grabbed the scythe with his left hand. The explosion of opposite charges was deafening as the scythe repelled his touch, but he didn't let go. Electricity flew in every direction, and like a net, it weaved its way up his hand and forearm, leaving behind a web of scorched skin. Lucifer forcefully pulled the scythe to him twisting it back and away from me at the same time. Then, he suddenly reverted the motion and shoved it back at me crashing the shaft into my skull. My eyes blacked out momentarily and I toppled over, letting go of my scythe as it clangored on the ground beside me.

From my position on the ground, I saw Lucifer standing almost with his back to me. He was holding his left hand and staring at his charred and smoking fingers. The shock to my head must have been massive since, although I could see the red of his eyes and knew that he would make me pay dearly for this, all I could think about was how unappetizing a barbequed devil's finger would be. Then, like a predator that had just remembered its prey, his head veered to me and with a determined pace he moved in for the kill. My scythe's steel blade was only a foot away, but there was no time for me to try to reach its shaft. I scrambled on all fours and grabbed it hastily, the blade's edge cutting through my palm and fingers to the bone. I gritted my teeth, holding in the crippling pain, and swung the scythe in a wide arc as the bloody blade started to slip through my fingers. Blood gushed across its edge, but I held on until it was on target and then let go with a gut wrenching roar. The scythe flew through the air like a boomerang straight for Lucifer's legs, but he did not flinch or miss a beat as he continued his charge. I knew the blade would slice right through him and for an instant it looked like it was over; that I could still make it to Kay in time. I looked at the passing images on the wall. To my dismay, the call was over and she was leaving the apartment.

Lucifer continued on the collision course without the slightest concern; his focus directed only at me. At the last instant, however, he effortlessly launched himself into the air like an arrow, did a somersault with scimitar in hand as my scythe flew past underneath him, and gracefully rolled on the ground and stood. Behind him, I saw the driver walk into the hall as Kay locked the door. That image was the catalyst I needed; it was now or never. Desperate and blind with fear, I lunged forward as Lucifer brought down the scimitar. Using my forearm, I diverted the blow and kneed him repeatedly in the gut. He doubled over, but at the same time slashed at my leg. I stepped back as the blade cut air and countered with a sequence of kicks and punches. Lucifer powerfully defended each blow, and it felt like I was hitting a pillar of stone. Neither of us stepped back, however, and we fell into a rhythm of synchronized attacks and defenses, neither breaking the other. I knew time was running out, but couldn't take the chance to take my eyes off of Lucifer to look at Kay. Suddenly, he jumped back, breaking the sequence, and sneered as he quickly glanced up at the makeshift screen. The driver was blocking Kay's path. Kay stopped and stared at him unfazed.

"It will be quite romantic to have you die with her. If taking a *single* life prematurely would be the end of you, I wonder what would happen if you killed thousands!" Lucifer dropped his scimitar and took a deep breath. I wasn't sure what he meant and just stared as he stretched his arms wide and then brought them together in a deafening clap. Fire exploded from his hands as thousands of candles flew off the mantles and whistled through the air like arrows straight at me. There was nowhere for me to hide or avoid the attack, and if only one of the candles touched my skin, that soul would be lost and so would I. I kneeled and unleashed my wings, forming them in front of me like a shield. Immediately, countless candle arrows pierced and shot through them, tearing and burning at the same time. The impact was formidable and sent me skidding backwards, but just as quickly, the fusillade was over. Then I heard another clap, just as thunderous, and was assaulted by a new wave of candles. My wings were practically gone, feathers and membrane burnt to the core, leaving only the skeletal structure that did not provide enough coverage to hide me. I was lucky that no souls were lost the first two rounds, but would not survive a third assault. Quickly, I bowed and pointed my wings forward. I was already numb to pain, and sacrificing my wings to try to save myself was the only option left. I pulled back the smoking structure and with great force, abruptly snapped it forward. Hundreds of featherless calami shot out at Lucifer like a deadly swarm of hornets. He dove to the side, but wasn't fast enough and was stabbed and pierced repeatedly by calamus after calamus as he crashed against the wall and fell to the ground motionless. The damage to his beastly figure was awesome and he looked even more grotesque than before; a red horned oozing porcupine. This was my chance to get out. I looked up and saw the driver take out a gun. I had to go! I turned and shot several fireballs at the collapsed ceiling where the door used to be. The explosion was massive, but it only opened enough of a passage for me to maybe squeeze through. I started to run, my only thoughts centered on Kay.

"Not so fast, little brother."

A red fireball flew over my head and crashed into the ceiling causing a large section of the wall to collapse. My passage to Kay was gone. I bellowed and turned back. Lucifer was standing where I last saw him, but now he was engulfed in flames. I guess it was easier to burn the calami rather than pick them out one by one. Above him, the driver was still pointing the gun at Kay, but somehow he looked distracted; his eyes less menacing.

"Nice move, little brother. Things are finally getting interesting with you and your tricks. I didn't know you could do that with your wings." Lucifer removed a calamus from his chest and used it to pick at his fangs. "But you're still not up to par with me."

"Me alone, maybe not. And you're right, I'm not up to par with you because I'm not like you. But, I'm also not alone and that makes me stronger." I pointed to the image of Kay on the wall and smiled. "Take a look."

Lucifer looked up just as Gabriel reached over and took the gun from the driver's hand. Although I didn't see or hear what happened, I knew Gabriel and unlike Michael and me he did not resort to force to get things done. He was calm and had the patience to talk, love and transform the soul. I smiled because I could not remember the last time Gabriel actually confronted anyone physically. How could he, in that ancient, ridiculous, white robe?

The driver threw himself at Gabriel, and although Gabriel was not particularly fond of physical contact, he embraced him.

"Friends and brothers," Lucifer chided, "always leeching off you and getting in the way. But, I guess they can be useful sometimes." Lucifer frowned and turned to look at me. "And predictable." He smiled and the wickedness of it chilled me to the bone. "It's time for my backup, backup plan." With that, he pointed to the driver and ordered, "Now!"

I don't know how the driver heard Lucifer, but they must have been connected, because he immediately locked his foot behind Gabriel's and pushed hard. Gabriel, trapped in the driver's embrace, lost his balance and they went crashing. I didn't understand how that was helpful, but then I saw him. It was the killer, the same man I had committed myself to destroy, and he was there to finish the job. I clenched my fists in dread, and the cold silence that engulfed my being was terrifying. The killer took out his gun and aimed at Kay.

Gabriel, still on the ground, lifted his arm in supplication. "Son, you don't want to do that." Gabriel's voice, so hollow and deep, resonated through me and I was shaken from the mist my mind had settled into. I glowered at Lucifer.

The killer tilted his gun sideways and stared at Gabriel in disbelief. "Oh, yes I do. You have no idea! Before, it was a job. Now, it's personal and I'm glad to comply."

"Do it, do it," slurped Lucifer in an almost singing tone.

The muffled sound of the gunshot exploded through my mind, and from the corner of my eye I saw Kay fall, but I didn't turn to look; I couldn't. My focus was Lucifer. All I wanted to do was to hurt – kill him. My pain would come later.

Lucifer, on the other hand, was caught in the ecstasy of his victory; his eyes reveled in my torment and despair, and he was basking in the fire of his hell, hoping to take me with him. I welcomed his arrogance and cockiness, because his inattention would be his demise. I closed my hand and summoned my scythe from where it lay on the ground behind him. It shot forward and spearheaded straight for his back, but Lucifer knew me well and was ready. Defending himself against a single attack that wasn't very stealthy didn't require much from him. In a mocking dance-like move he spun around and kicked the scythe away.

"Here's *my* backup plan, asshole!" With that, I lifted my arms and fired at him indiscriminately. Lucifer turned just in time to dodge the first fireball, but the rest were on target. Stubbornly, he held his ground, making each impact even more destructive than the one before. He roared louder and louder as his beastly form was punished until he finally fell to his knees. I stopped and looked at him, but there was no mercy in me; only justice as I saw it. I walked to him and grabbed him by the neck as he had done with me and threw him hard against the wall. He tried to stand but was too spent and again fell to the floor on his hands and knees. Once more, in a state of uncontrolled rage, I fired fireball after fireball, but this time at the wall above him. When the barrage was over, not much was left of the wall and Lucifer was on the ground buried in the rubble. I walked over and stood over him. He looked pathetic and broken, but I still wasn't content. I bent over, grabbed him by the neck again and pulled him from the destruction without consideration for his wounds. He didn't call out or show any pain. Instead, he smiled.

"You lost, brother. You lost her for a second time."

Still holding Lucifer by the neck, I reached behind me with my free hand and grabbed the remains of my wing. With a powerful twist, I broke off the long bone that connected the wing structure to my back and held it in front of him. Its sides were jagged and the end sharp and pointed.

"To get the *rose*, you have to *respect* the thorn. *This* is for Kay and Martha," I hissed, and thrust the bone through Lucifer, impaling him to what remained of the wall.

Lucifer's ferocious cry filled the room. He looked down at the bone extruding from his stomach and grabbed it with both hands. His snake-like tongue slithered out and he hissed, "Are you done having fun, yet?"

"I'm getting there." I turned and summoned my scythe. "Now, unlike you, *I'm* going to end it all!" I placed the edge of the scythe against Lucifer's neck and fixed my eyes his. "I hope you have friends where you're going." I swung the scythe around my head and brought it across in a perfect arc. Inches away from hitting its mark, its blade clanged loudly against the edge of a mighty sword and was blocked. I turned knowing well who to expect.

"How dare you?" I dropped the scythe and grabbed Michael by the arms, lifting him off the ground and throwing him against the wall beside Lucifer. "*You* killed her. If you had just stayed out of it…"

"Azrail, look!" Michael yelled and pointed.

Maybe it is true and hope *is* the last thing to die, but I still didn't want to look at the scene on the wall. I didn't want to see Kay. Then, I heard Gabriel's voice come booming through, "Screw this! No one listens to me anymore!" I looked up just in time to see him, the peace loving angel of Man, grab the killer and throw him clear across the hall.

I looked back at Michael and said in a feral tone, "You stopped me for this?"

"No, Az, he stopped you for me." Kay's voice ripped through me. I let go of Michael and dropped to my knees. There was nothing to say as I looked up and saw Kay standing over me, her young face brilliant but concerned. And there, behind her stood Gabriel, once again serene and composed. I felt my eyes burn with tears, both of exhaustion and great joy, because in my heart I finally knew that Kay was going to be okay, not because of me, but because of us.

Lucifer's pitiful groan caught my attention and I turned. "Someone get this damn bird away from me and get me off of this thing…"

The sight of Bran hopping around Lucifer cawing at him made me smile. He was saying screw you in bird language. I looked at Michael and he shrugged, so I stood up and complied. With a swift tug, I pulled out the bone spear and Lucifer crumbled to the ground.

"You know, I defaced you once before and that wasn't angelic. I think I should fix it now, you devious, old snake. How about something more symmetrical?"

Lucifer stared up at me and let out a threatening snarl as I lifted my foot. "Don't! You have no idea."

The threat was lost amidst the explosion of red energy as my booted foot crashed down on his right horn, smashing it into pieces. "Actually, I do, but somehow I doubt things can get any worse between us, brother."

I looked down at Lucifer as he rocked from side-to-side moaning in pain. Slowly, his horn started to regenerate. "I think I goofed. The scars on your horns won't be symmetrical after all."

THIRTY

I stood on the ledge of the same building where I dropped the killer and stared over the city. The night was dark, but there was no rain or thunder, just the sounds of life as Man went about his business. *"How oblivious can they be?"* I thought to myself and hung my head.

I saw my chest and arms, a reminder of the hell I had just come from. They were covered with cuts and bruises, and my muscles burned and complained as I passed my hand over my cheek and neck. Every movement was filled with agony, but strangely it felt good. It was a reminder that I had survived where I shouldn't have. My awe inspiring look, however, was nothing but abhorrent – bloody and disheveled – and my overcoat was so torn and tattered that it barely stayed put on my shoulders. But there was no rage or anger, just a feeling of emptiness. Kay survived and would always survive. She had the light, that nobility that Gabriel always talked about. But what about the rest of Man? Was this the world I was committed to? A multitude of greedy souls going about doing what's best for themselves and narrowly missing the ride to hell because of me? Because Father is merciful and always gives Man a second chance? I shrugged. It didn't matter, I was tired and would probably feel better tomorrow.

Bran landed on my right shoulder and cawed gently. I glanced at him but didn't smile. I didn't feel like it. My emotions were null, a complete void. He cawed again, this time louder. Obviously, he wanted my attention. I brushed him off my shoulder.

"Not now, Bran. I'm too tired."

He shrieked and landed on my shoulder again, and pulled my ear to the right with his beak. I felt anger stir inside me, but then I saw a brightly shining light in the distance and my heart filled with sad happiness. It was my light, my Kay. What was she up to? And then, I saw another light, and another, and another… and they slowly scattered all over. I closed my eyes and felt a strange warmth encompass me and smiled. Yes, I *was* committed to Man.

"Man is defined by his roots, but in the end his noble essence will always

triumph."

With my help, of course!

THE END

NOTE FROM THE AUTHOR:

I truly hope that you enjoyed reading Az as much as I enjoyed writing it.

Before putting the book or your Kindle aside, I humbly ask that you please

take a moment to leave a review on Amazon. Reader reviews are very

important to me and help the books you like become more popular. I've

included a link below for your convenience. Thank you!

https://www.amazon.com/review/create-review/?asin=1512076902

Dear reader,

Thank you for reading *Az – Revenge of an Archangel.* I hope that you enjoyed the ride as much as I enjoyed writing it. Please feel free to contact me with any remarks or questions about the story, characters, or whatever detail which may have caught your attention or interest. I enjoy getting feedback and do my best to answer.

As you may know, for self-published and independent authors, gaining exposure is almost more difficult than writing the book. It mostly relies on word of mouth and the kindness of readers to tell their friends and family. This being said, if you have the time and desire to do so, I would be most appreciative if you would consider leaving a short review on Amazon or wherever you feel is most convenient.

Warmest regards,
A. A. Bavar
www.aabavar.com
aabavar@aabavar.com

SAMANTHA

by A. A. Bavar
(based on a story by Scott Spotson)
cover art by Sarah Bavar
edited by Natalie Bavar

SUMMARY
Bewitched meets Fatal Attraction

Nothing is as it seems where Samantha is involved:
The mysterious theft of the Hope Diamond by Marie Antoinette…
The daring heist of an original Van Gogh by the Joker…
Falling in love with the perfect man…

Patricia Fowler, a young executive scraping to make it to the top, meets the mysterious and alluring Paul Blast. He offers her a fast pass to success, but is finding the perfect man and getting your dream job worth facing off against Samantha? For Patricia, it's the razor edge between what could be and insanity.

Security guard Walter Brodsky watched disinterestedly as the usual throng of curious visitors circled the Hope Diamond display. He smirked and allowed his eyes to roam the room, looking for anything out of the ordinary. Anything to keep him awake.

"Damn, when Joe told me this was an easy job he should have warned me about the Valium effect. Eight freakin' months and nothing but some rowdy kids and a crazy schmuck with a diamond fetish," he mumbled to himself, shaking his head. "I really hope something interesting happens one of these days… anything!"

"Be careful what you wish for, mon ami," warned a soft, gentle voice to Walter's right.

Walter turned and was surprised to see a woman in a wide hat with long blue and pink feathers, wearing a loose white gown with a colorful sash around the waist, looking at him. "Excuse me?" he said, lifting his eyebrows in surprise.

The woman didn't respond; but smiled coquettishly and walked away.

"Man, I need a break from the crazies," Walter said as he rubbed the back of his neck, his eyes following the eccentric woman until she disappeared behind one of the columns. He shrugged and continued his lazy walk around the room, his mind wandering to his plans for the weekend and the Redskins' game with his buddies. The problem was that he hadn't told his wife, and she wanted him to refinish the kitchen cabinets. Walter frowned, Tammy's ultimatum from that morning fresh in his mind. *You know the money we've been saving to finish the basement? The ultimate man cave you've been boasting about to your buddies? Well, you can kiss it goodbye if these cabinets aren't sparkling by Monday, 'cause I've already chosen new ones and all I have to do is click the purchase button!*

"No way that's gonna happen," he grumbled to himself. "I'll stay up all night if I have to, and those deadbeats are gonna come and help."

A smile slowly crept across Walter's lips as he imagined his finished basement, a fully stocked bar with a beer tap, a 60 inch high definition TV with Bose surround sound, a pool table, leather couch, two lazy boys, and – suddenly, the ear splitting shriek of the alarm system brought Walter crashing back to the present. His gaze instantly snapped to the Hope Diamond even though he knew the multi-million dollar security system at the Smithsonian was virtually fool-proof. As he expected, the marble base was rapidly descending into the floor, and the display with the diamond would soon be secured in an impenetrable underground vault. But where the hell was the Hope Diamond?

Walter rushed forward in shock as the opening in the floor started to close over the empty display. His head jerked from side to side seeking out the stone, a thief, anything out of place. But there was nothing. In disbelief, he looked down at the recessed floor one last time before the opening slammed shut. To his surprise the Hope Diamond was back inside the glass display.

"What the hell?"

"Your eyes have played a trick on you, mon ami," said the same soft, gentle voice from before. "But now, your day has become a bit more exciting. No?"

Walter spun around, but the woman in the oddly lavish outfit was nowhere near him. He turned from side to side and finally saw her standing by the exit door of the Annenberg Hooker Hall as if waiting for him to look. She smiled, waved in a queenly fashion, and walked away.

2

Patricia Fowler's toned body cut through the water with exceptional grace. Her movements were fluid, almost dolphin-like as she took in stroke after stroke towards the end of the pool. She was the image of perfection, a sort of clean, natural attractiveness combined with a focused mind and an athletic body. As she closed in on the wall in front of her, her body twisted into a perfect flip, her feet coming into contact with its smooth ceramic surface and propelling her in the opposite direction. As Patricia surfaced, she seamlessly transitioned from forward crawl to breaststroke, the next phase in her practice session.

13... 14... 15... 16... 17... I gotta stop counting all my strokes. When did I become so anal, she thought, but as much as Patricia tried to she couldn't stop herself from mentally reviewing every aspect of her routine. Thirty-six laps every session neatly divided into rounds by stroke type: front crawl, breaststroke, backstroke, and inverted breaststroke. For the umpteenth time, she thought about adding another four laps to make it a round forty. *No,* she insisted to herself. *I don't want to push it too hard. I'm in a sweet spot now. It's been a year of perfection. Why change?*

Patricia smirked and continued forward, a well-oiled machine doing what it was designed to do. She followed the same routine every week: Mondays, Wednesdays, and Fridays were dedicated to swimming while Tuesdays and Thursdays were for jogging. Becoming a member of the fitness facility across from her office at Clearwell, Inc. was a spur of the moment decision, but with her job as a high-level marketing manager it turned out to be the best thing she could have done. Swimming grounded and relaxed her, while running made her robust and boosted her confidence. Occasionally on Fridays, however, her co-workers would ask her to join them for lunch in the park next to the office, and she always said yes. It was a way for her to fit in so as not to be viewed as one of those solitary types who eventually got shunned by the group. Besides, she liked her co-workers and certainly needed more social activity in her life, which lately revolved mostly around work and workouts. She hadn't had a serious relationship in four years, and it was time to start looking again even if it meant having co-workers suggest brothers, cousins, and even second-cousins as potential love interests. Apparently, twenty-seven was the new twenty-two, the perfect age for finding someone and settling down.

Patricia almost laughed, it was such an antiquated thought. And the makeup and dresses they suggested she wear, it was crazy. She took great pride in her natural femininity, and the old-fashioned approach to beauty made her skin crawl. She didn't need hundreds of dollars of creamy enhancements, or three hour sessions at the hairdresser. She was tall, slender, and attractive and that's what she wanted to show. At most, she used her long, sleek, chestnut hair to nicely frame her face and on occasion added the most subtle lipstick or eyeliner. The right man would find her eventually.

No rush, she told herself. *Focus on paying off the mortgage. Focus on your career. Let things happen.* She closed her eyes and kicked hard. As the water streamed past her, the image of the perfect man invaded her thoughts. A confident yet sensitive guy with no emotional baggage, a sturdy body, and rugged features. Someone tender and mysterious who you must surrender to in a lifelong journey while falling deeply in love. That's what she wanted. She was done with the pudgy clingy type, the unmotivated slob, or the anal-retentive and emotionally obtuse.

Patricia's outstretched fingertips scraped the edge of the pool, snapping her out of her daydream. She stopped and looked towards the clock on the wall at the other end of the room. Instead, all she saw was a tower of well-defined legs. Her eyes slowly made their way up the chiseled body of the man looming above her, and she gasped as they finally landed on the face looking down at her. The man's sleek, jet black hair was pulled back into a tight ponytail like a professional platform diver or a mysterious Flamenco dancer. Either way, he was the perfect example of raw masculinity, a kind of magnetic pull that had Patricia gaping like a teenager.

"I believe you're done," said the man. He was holding out a towel for her, but didn't offer to help her out of the pool.

"Huh? Oh, yes, I guess I am," she said, and climbed out. She stood there dripping for a moment before taking the towel. "I'm actually not quite done. I mean, I'm done with the pool, but was going to—"

"The hot tub. I know," interrupted the man.

"Aren't you—"

"Paul Blast? Yes, I am," he said with a grin. "And believe me, I'm not a stalker. I've been coming here for a few weeks, actually. But you're so focused on your routine that you never noticed. I like that."

"I'm so sorry, Mr. Blast," blurted Patricia. She was trying hard not to look down at Paul's chest and toned abs. After all, he was one of the directors at Clearwell, her boss's boss; John's boss.

"No worries. Like I said, I admire your determination. I noticed you never change your routine in the slightest, just the intensity, and that tells me a lot." Paul stopped and frowned. "I guess I am a stalker of sorts."

"No! No! I understand," said Patricia.

"Just kidding," said Paul with a slight chuckle, then added in a more serious tone, "Mind if I join you in the hot tub?"

Patricia felt her head reel for a split second. She blinked slowly, her brown eyes focusing on the face in front of her. Instinctively, she nodded and smiled. Paul's deep, blue eyes smiled back.

"Sure, of course," she said in a much calmer and confident tone than she felt. It was a trick she had mastered when giving presentations, to appear in control even when the situation was beyond your control.

Patricia turned and headed for the hot tub, but watched Paul from the corner of her eye as he followed. *What does he want? How could I have not noticed him all these weeks? But then, why would I?* She reached the tub, climbed the steps, and slid into the water. As usual, the hot water immediately soothed and relaxed her.

When she turned, Paul was standing on the edge of the hot tub, tall, lean and confident. He paused momentarily, one hand on the railing, his eyes watching her every move, before stepping down into the pool. Almost immediately, the relaxed feeling she had experienced just a moment before vanished, and she could feel her heart beating frenetically through her chest. She watched as his body slowly disappeared into the water, and for a fleeting moment an image of him wearing a tie over his bare chest popped into her mind. *What the hell are you thinking? Are you trying to get fired?* Patricia shook her head, leaned back, and closed her eyes. Hopefully he would be gone when she reopened them.

"Patricia, do you mind if I ask you a question?" asked Paul as he settled down on the submerged bench, the water up to just below his shoulders.

Patricia opened her eyes, her heart in her mouth. Paul was the director of the Brand Management group, and she only knew him by sight. He seldom came down to her floor, but she had heard that he was a hard and meticulous worker and expected the same dedication from everyone. No one really knew much about his personal life, but it was common knowledge that he had risen very quickly in the ranks and was headed to the top. There was even talk of him as the new Vice-President of the department.

"Um, sure," she said, and broke into a friendly smile. There was a warm flutter in her chest, and she felt it crawl up her neck to her face. *What's happening? I'm too young for a hot flash,* she thought as she forced herself to keep a straight face.

"How committed are you to Clearwell? And before you answer that, are you available for dinner tonight?" asked Paul in an almost formal tone. He leaned back placing his elbows on the edge of the tub.

"I'm sorry, what? I don't quite understand."

Paul smiled and held up his hand apologetically. "Sorry, didn't mean to ambush you with two questions. Let me start over. I've been hearing very complimentary things about your work and want to know how you see your future at Clearwell. As for the second question," Paul paused and grinned sheepishly, "I can't lie. Dinner wouldn't be solely for business. You intrigue me, and I would love to get to know you better."

Patricia was silent for a moment, her composure as professional as possible under the circumstances. Then, as she was about to respond, an image of Paul wearing only his swimming trunks and a tie while sitting at a table in a very fancy restaurant invaded her thoughts. "You must be kidding me!" she said choking over her words. Then, before Paul could respond, added, "Sorry, I didn't mean to say that. I just had a strange thought… and this is so unusual."

"Don't worry about it, my fault. I overstepped," said Paul, then added with a smile. "Let me make it up to you with dinner?"

Patricia glanced at her hands resting on her knees under the water. The skin was getting wrinkled; it was time to leave. "I'm sorry, but I don't think it's a good idea," she said, and stood up.

"Fair enough, but please, don't go. I do want to hear your goals at Clearwell." Paul gestured for her to sit.

Patricia looked at the clock on the wall. It was 12:55. "I would love to discuss it with you, Mr. Blast, but I'm going to be late as it is."

"Don't worry about it. If anyone asks, tell them you were in a meeting with me. And Patricia, please call me Paul."

There was a moment's hesitation before Patricia smiled gently and sat back down. "Okay, Paul, what would you like to know?"

"Basically, how hard are you willing to push your career at Clearwell?"

Patricia reached up and brushed away a strand of hair that had strayed across her eye. "As hard as necessary. I believe that my work speaks for itself."

"Yes, it does, and John speaks very highly of you." Paul sat forward, putting his arms back in the water and resting his elbows on his knees. Patricia's eyes followed the movement and came to rest on Paul's crotch. "So, my question is would you be open to a departmental change for faster growth opportunities? At first, it would be a horizontal shift from your current position, but I guarantee…"

Jesus, Mary, and Joseph, control yourself! Patricia looked up at Paul, her eyebrows arching up in confusion. *What did he just say? A horizontal what?*

"Patricia? Are you okay?" asked Paul.

"Yes, yes, of course. I just wasn't quite sure what you meant by a horizontal…"

"Shift," completed Paul. "It means you will keep your title as manager but work in my department on a new project I'm launching. I want you to spearhead that project."

"So I'll be working with you?"

"Not directly, but yes. Steve Browski is the managing director for the department, but since I know he's being considered for a promotion…" Paul smiled without finishing the sentence.

"I see," said Patricia. "This really is unexpected, considering where we are."

"Unexpected things can be good."

A sly smile spread across Patricia's lips. "Yes, they can, thank you. But I need a day or two to think it over. Can you wait?"

"Only if you give me the answer over dinner."

Patricia shook her head and smiled. "You know where my office is," she said, standing to leave. "I'll let you know."

Paul nodded.

Patricia hopped out of the hot tub, took a few steps, and then doubled back, colliding headfirst into a heavyset man who was walking past her. As she bounced off his large belly, the man grabbed her to keep her from slipping.

"Oh my goodness, I'm so sorry!" she exclaimed and hurried away without looking back.

Buy now:

https://www.amazon.com/dp/B0762H1T7W/

COMING SOON

by A. A. Bavar

SHUTDOWN

We once vowed there would never

be another 9/11

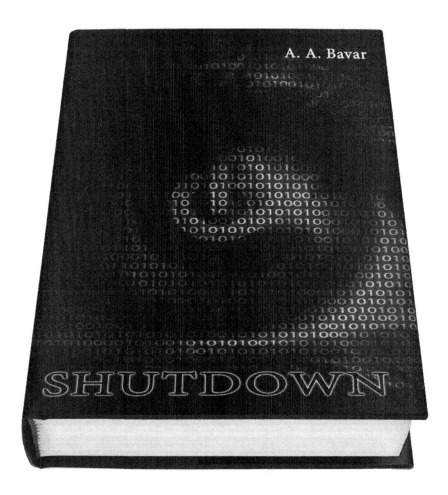

Sarah Bavar

Artist / Illustrator

www.sarahbavar.com

Printed in Great Britain
by Amazon

41352511R00145